WALLFLOWER

heidi belleau

RIPTIDE
PUBLISHING

Riptide Publishing
PO Box 6652
Hillsborough, NJ 08844
www.riptidepublishing.com

Wallflower (Rear Entrance Video, #2)

Cover art: Vivian Ng, viivus.tumblr.com
Editor: Sarah Frantz Lyons
Layout: L.C. Chase, lcchase.com/design.htm

ISBN: 978-1-62649-037-6

First edition
October, 2013

Also available in ebook:
ISBN: 978-1-62649-036-9

WALLFLOWER

heidi belleau

RIPTIDE
PUBLISHING

table of
contents

CHAPTER 1

Rob breathed through the sun salutation, trying his damnedest to exhale out all the tension still clenching the muscles of his back and shoulders. It used to be that the weekly yoga class he took with his big sister could get him through anything: any stressor, any sadness, any frustration, any loneliness . . . but today, not so much.

Give it a chance, he coaxed himself. Inhale. Exhale.

Nope, totally not working. He couldn't get the thought of tonight off his mind.

His first shift alone at Rear Entrance Video, and he couldn't have felt less prepared—and more anxious—if he'd tried. Oh, he had plenty of experience after the last two months working shifts with Christian supervising; he knew how to work the rental system and count out the till, knew the layout of the store, knew his Jenna Jameson from his James Deen, could even recite the myriad benefits of silicone as a material for use in sex toys.

What he *couldn't* do was picture himself working alone and one-on-one with a stranger—a customer, no less—doing any of those things. Especially not the "sexy" stuff. Which, of course, when you worked at a porn store meant pretty much everything, since even routine activities like filing took on new and terrifying X-rated meanings.

He startled when a hand touched the back of his left thigh—speaking of risqué. "Downward-facing dog," the class's willowy blonde instructor said, obviously repeating herself. She planted her other hand on his lower back to guide him down. His palms hit the mat and he let out a violent gust of air. "Ujjayi breath," she reminded him, and although she talked as softly and as calmly as ever, Rob could hear displeasure there too, no doubt at the fact that he'd brought his distraction and stress into her studio.

"Child's pose," she said, louder, as she mercifully drifted away.

Now that one he could do, and gladly. He sank down, curling in on himself, letting his forehead rest on the soft fabric of the mat, his hair falling in a black curtain that shielded him from the outside world.

Child's pose—that was the perfect name for it, because he wished he could stay this way forever. But of course he couldn't, and before he knew it they were all putting their hands together and bowing as their instructor murmured, "Namaste."

In the time it took Rob to pick up his water bottle and take a swig, his sister was already surrounded by a chatty group of lithe men and women all competing for her attention. Rob sighed, shook his head, and forced his sore thighs into a squat so he could roll up his mat.

Bernice had been the one to suggest the yoga classes, back when she'd been in her last year of high school and Rob had just been starting. Her rationale back then had been that it was an activity they could do together, where the socially awkward caterpillar and the social butterfly could find common ground. But Rob had always suspected a hidden motive of it being an activity that required Rob to get out of the house and be around people, even if all they were doing was waggling their butts in the air. Whatever her motivations, Rob had agreed to go along just to make her happy, and then later agreed to keep going because getting out apparently made *him* happy, too, and he wanted more of that. He'd committed to it. To her. To himself.

Give her way a chance. Mat under one arm and water bottle hooked around one finger, he squared his shoulders and walked over.

The circle of admirers didn't shift, so Rob cleared his throat. Shook his bangs out of his eyes and cleared his throat again.

He could stand around all day doing this before any of Bernice's beautiful crowd noticed him, but luckily a gorgeous muscular blond guy happened to shift a little on his bare feet, which made just enough of an opening for Bernice's eyes to land on Rob from over the blond's shoulder.

"Robby!" she said, and that was all it took for her friends to open up a space for him. He stepped into the circle with a shrug and a little half-smile. "You guys know my baby brother? How's it going, Robby? I saw Alyssa had to correct your poses. You weren't distracted staring at somebody's butt, were you?" She winked and flashed him a big, bright, pinup girl smile to show she was just teasing. At that, everyone laughed, and Rob wheezed out a little "Ha-ha," trying to hide his flush at the realization that he'd been behind a man in class today.

All this talk of butts and asses and Rear Entrances, was this seriously his life? Maybe he should stick to Kingdom of Elves for his socialization; at least there it was everybody else making all the crude commentary. At least there he had a screen to hide his blush behind.

If he were a more bitter person, he'd resent his sister for hogging all the beauty and charisma genes in the family and leaving him with nothing, but the truth was, he kind of suspected that she'd been born, heard her dowdy grandma name, and spent her whole life busting her butt to break that mould. So it wasn't a matter of not enough charm to go around, just the cold reality of which of them wanted it bad enough to work for it. And Bernice had worked. Hard, all her life. Sure, when they'd been teenagers it hadn't *seemed* like work when she'd pored over fashion magazines for the latest trends or spent an hour and a half in the bathroom every morning doing her hair and makeup, and it definitely hadn't seemed like work when she'd gone out with someone or other every night. Now that he was older, though, he realized that what he'd seen as play and fucking around had all been a concerted effort to become a person people liked and wanted to be around.

Rob, on the other hand, had spent more than a few years convincing himself of the exact opposite: that he didn't want or need anybody, no approval, no friends, nothing. That he was socially awkward and a loser, sure, but that it was better that way. Teenage Rob hadn't had friends because he didn't *need* friends. He was better off alone.

That had been before Emily Carr University, before Noah Hadley and his other roommates, *definitely* before Rear Entrance Video, and Rob liked to believe he was a changed man, at least as far as acknowledging his need for human companionship went, but he still had some catching-up to do.

Bernice shifted from one foot to the other. "So anyway, we were thinking of going for some smoothies. You in?" She and her friends all stared at Rob. Oh God, she was inviting him out. Again. Every week like clockwork she asked him to come out with her and her friends, and every week he panicked and refused, right back to being an insecure teenager again.

Okay, so maybe he had a *lot* of catching-up to do before he was a normal social human being like her.

They were all staring at him, Bernice hopeful, the others neutral at best, the gorgeous blond guy looking specifically unimpressed. Never mind Rob, this asshole obviously hadn't gotten the memo yet that high school was over. Rob turned from him, focusing on Bernice instead: her open expression, her fresh skin, her bangs spiking up where her Lululemon headband had slipped.

"Thanks for the invite, but I . . ." Bernice's face fell, and it almost broke Rob's heart, knowing he was disappointing her, knowing that he was kind of disappointing himself, too. Maybe, given time, he could prove the blond wrong. Probably not, but stranger things had happened. Stranger things . . . like Rear Entrance Video. "I can't. I promised to do one of my roommates a favor."

That seemed to cheer her up a little: helping a roommate probably sounded a lot more normal and social to her than his usual excuses of "I've got a raid," or just straight up "Not my scene."

The circle closed around her again, unconsciously-or-maybe-not shoving Rob out as they suggested the best nearby smoothie places, argued over vegan options and independent spots versus franchises, debated the merits of organic fruit. Vancouver talk. Rob let himself fall back in a subtle retreat, raising a hand in good-bye.

"See you next week?" Bernice asked, tilting her head at him with an expression that was half hope and half sadness. She wanted better for Rob. She always had. It was just too bad Rob wasn't quite ready to take that final step.

"Yeah, you know it," Rob said, forcing some cheerful enthusiasm into his voice, and Bernice smiled at him one last time before she turned back to her friends.

A short trip back to the house for a shower and a change of clothes, and Rob was on his way, hopping the bus down to Davie Street before he could change his mind.

Not that he *would* change his mind, of course. His roommates were counting on him. Not just Christian, who was the reason they were all working at Rear Entrance Video in the first place, but the others too: Max and Noah and Austin, who had all taken time out of their hectic lives to help Christian manage his aunt's store and depended on Rob to do his fair share, too. His . . . well, maybe it was presumptuous to call them "friends." Rob didn't have friends—not the way Bernice always had—but roommates on good terms, roommates he played video games and had midnight dinners with. Yeah, that. Whatever they were, Rob didn't want to let them down. He wanted them to like him, to be happy with him, to think he was a person who could be trusted, a person worth inviting along and including. And if a few shifts of awkwardness at a porn store was the price of their approval, then so be it.

Yeah. Rob could do this. Hell, maybe he'd like it. Meet new people. Learn new things.

He rang for his stop and, when the bus pulled to the curb, hopped out the door. Quickly glanced away from an attractive middle-aged bear who flashed him a smile as they passed each other on the sidewalk.

God, it was just a smile, not a pickup line. He needed to get himself together.

He pushed through the front door of the shop and waved to Christian, who was sitting behind the counter, and Max, who was perched *on* it like some kind of skater-boy lounge singer.

"Hey Rob," Christian greeted, and it heartened Rob to see that the gaunt, tormented look he'd been wearing the last couple months was finally starting to fade. He still had bags under his eyes, but that didn't necessarily mean a bad thing. After all, if Rob had Max for a boyfriend, he'd probably be having his fair share of late nights, too.

"How's it going, Nugget?" Max said. "Ready for your trial by fire?"

"Max, don't be a dick," Christian snapped, then turned a slightly feral grin on Rob. "Don't worry, Rob, I got all the creepers out of the way this afternoon. Should be smooth sailing tonight."

"Oh, you can schedule them now?" Rob's tone was sarcastic as he slipped behind the counter and kicked his bag underneath it. He took his seat next to Christian, who immediately popped the till drawer for changeover.

Max threw a look over his shoulder at them both. "Yeah, didn't you hear? Noon to one, Christian does creeper hour: creepy customers get all rentals half off. Gets 'em out of the way."

"He's joking, right?" Rob asked, playing along.

"Hmm." Christian didn't look up from the bills he was passing from hand to hand as he counted in his head. "I'd say so, but who knows what he gets up to when I'm not here. Maybe he just wants to hog all the creepers to himself."

"You got me. Although truth be told, it's all a ploy to get at the only creeper that matters: Sweatpants-and-boner Guy." Max batted his eyelashes, putting his chin in his hands like a smitten teenage girl.

"He's all yours." Rob shuddered. Although ninety percent of their clientele were completely normal—drunk college students, groups of women looking for satin blindfolds and rabbit pearls, friendly dudes, shy and awkward types like Rob himself—there was that last ten percent, the ones with boundary issues, the ones without personal hygiene . . .

Sweatpants-and-boner Guy was an obese, middle-aged man—nothing wrong with that part, of course—who came in wearing baggy sweatpants that clung to his boner as he wandered the aisles licking and smacking his lips. He was completely harmless, but everybody who worked the counter wished he'd invest in some jeans or something, *anything* to even somewhat hide the chubby he always sported.

The cash register slammed shut. "Well, that's it for me, I'm outta here," Christian said. "Ready to go, babe? Rob, you're gonna be okay here on your own?"

"Yeah," Rob said, pushing all of his insecurities down into the bottom of his gut. Just because he was being a ridiculous baby about all this didn't mean he had to show it. "Go on, get out of here. I'll call you if anything goes wrong."

Christian dropped a hand onto Rob's shoulder in that overearnest teacher way he sometimes did. "Nothing's going to go wrong, Rob. You'll be just fine."

Jeez, had he been that obvious?

He shrugged Christian's hand off, not quite confident enough in his lying ability to meet Christian's eyes. "Sure, sure, sure. Now go."

Christian cast him one more dopey, concerned look, then got up, took Max's hand, and let Max lead him out the door. When the bell jingled their exit, Rob sighed with relief, slumping in his chair. Alone. Finally. Was it wrong to wish he'd be alone all night?

Considering they were trying to get the store up and running for Christian's cancer patient aunt, who owned the place and had managed it before she got sick, yeah, it really was.

And in some cosmic and/or divine punishment for his selfishness, the doorbell jingled again—from the back of the store, this time, the titular Rear Entrance—and in walked the only customer higher (or was that lower?) on the hierarchy of creepers than Sweatpants-and-boner Guy: Charlie VIP. No last name on file, just "VIP," probably because if you looked into his customer history he had a perfect rental record and had spent the price of a pretty damn decent new car here over the last year or so. Guess that bought a little discretion when it came to last names and phone numbers.

It wasn't that he was rude or abusive, exactly, more just . . . incredibly uncomfortable to be around. "Evenin'," he greeted on his way to the Fetish section of the store.

"Hello," Rob mumbled to the counter, ducking his eyes behind his hair. *He's harmless*, he reminded himself. *He probably looks creepier than he actually is.* He thought of himself, the way people treated him based solely on outward appearances. How they judged him. Not that he wasn't a completely average Chinese Canadian teenage boy, from the cheap Hong Kong fashion right up to the shaggy K-pop haircut. But the way he spoke, the way he carried himself . . . people picked up on that, he had to assume, picked up on it and read *doormat* and *nerd* and *loser* and that's what he was to them, whether he wanted to be that person or not. And eventually, what they thought of him had become the truth, a self-fulfilling prophecy that he couldn't seem to escape.

Maybe it was the same for Charlie VIP.

Or maybe he really was just a creepy pervert, as advertised.

Rob risked a glance at Charlie VIP and quickly ducked behind the computer monitor again before the guy caught him looking. Fuzzy slippers, like Grampa Simpson. A white cabled cardigan, open to the third button like Mr. Rogers, but with nothing underneath except for chest hair and the occasional glimpse of old-dude nipple. Wild, thinning hair. Scabby cold sores around the corner of his mouth. The guy looked like a textbook addict, except in this case his drug of choice was porno rather than heroin or meth.

In other words, he looks like a guy who doesn't need your judgment.

As resolved as Rob was, though, he still couldn't meet the guy's eye when he came up to the counter with a stack of German medical fetish and fisting movies. The women in this German stuff the distributor sent them always looked so haggard and skinny and pale, but maybe that was just because Rob had become acclimatized to the California version of sexuality, women with tans and fake tits and perfect makeup and nails.

"Find everything you were looking for?" he forced himself to ask.

Charlie drummed his fingers on the countertop like he was antsy for his fix. "You need more midget stuff." He spoke with a growl, but there was no anger in his face. Maybe he just had a worn voice, although he didn't smell of cigarette smoke. Maybe he'd quit. Traded one addiction for another less likely to kill him. "I seen this one eight times."

Nine times, actually. Rob couldn't think of anything more awkward and uncomfortable than making small talk with this guy about midget porn, so he didn't say anything at all, just popped the empty cases onto the OUT shelf and went rooting through the filing cabinet for Charlie's discs.

"Thanks, kid. You tell your manager about them midgets."

Rob saluted him, which seemed to work just as well as speaking. Good thing too, because he wasn't sure he *could* speak. Or at least, not without squeaking like a pubescent boy.

Another sigh of relief at the sound of the doorbell, but when Rob looked up, Charlie was still loitering around looking at the blow-up dolls. Coming through the door now was a big Native guy, probably Max and Christian's age, wearing one of those black and red ERASE RACISM NAZI PUNKS FUCK OFF sweatshirts that Rob was pretty sure were for some metal band, although he did appreciate the sentiment, wherever it came from.

ERASE RACISM guy had the hood pulled up over his head, though, and no amount of chiding himself about not judging people by appearances could keep Rob from reacquainting himself with the location of the panic button underneath the counter.

Charlie seemed to feel the same way, because he clutched his plain black plastic bag to his chest and scurried out without a word.

A few minutes later, ERASE RACISM guy sauntered up to the counter with a big grin, put down a DVD case, and pulled the hood from his head.

Hood down, he transformed into a teddy bear with a round face and twinkling black eyes. His wet bangs flopped forward until he peevishly raked them back again.

Oh, it had been raining outside. Thus the hood. Duh.

Rob spared a passing thought for Charlie in his slippers. He hoped the guy had a car somewhere nearby.

"Didja get a load of that guy?" ERASE RACISM said, and handed over his membership card. Dylan Ford, age twenty-three.

"Um . . . Not really . . ." Rob mumbled, and turned for the filing cabinets before Dylan could see the flush on his face.

He hoped the conversation would end there, but it didn't. "Not like I can talk, right?" Dylan laughed. "Guy my age coming to a porno store for anything but a prank, weird, right?"

"I don't know. Maybe. I guess."

"Is it bad that I feel the need to justify myself to you? Do you get that a lot? Dudes just coming in here giving you all these excuses for why they gotta rent porn? I bet you've heard some pretty good ones. Even though you probably don't care, right?" *Got it in one, buddy, not that it's going to stop you, I'm guessing.* And sure enough, Dylan continued, "Well, anyway, mine is that my parents get a copy of my credit card statements. This way I can pay cash." He gestured to the crinkled five dollar bill he'd put on the counter next to his DVD case. A gay DVD. Rob supposed that was a good reason to keep it from your parents . . . beyond just the embarrassment of having to explain the eighty-dollar charge from STR8 BOYS GONE GAY, INC. on your statement. "Not that I'm some closet case or something!" Dylan added with a scandalized expression, as if waiting to come out was some unheard-of thing, too sad and old-fashioned to comprehend.

"Mom and Dad know I'm a homo, but doesn't mean they need to know the details of what I jack off to, right?"

"Um, right," Rob said. *Although apparently it's fine if I know what you jack off to.*

Well, duh, because it's your job, you judgmental jerk. Feeling sorry, now, Rob managed a genuine smile for the guy. Just because Dylan's overfamiliarity made Rob feel embarrassed as hell didn't mean he had the right to be a douche about it.

Dylan smiled back, encouraged, and put both elbows on the counter as he watched Rob process the rental. "And my sister does porn in California so I'd feel bad pirating it."

God, was that supposed to be small talk? Did this guy not have a filter? All of Rob's goodwill washed away in a tidal wave of fresh awkwardness. He hummed a noncommittal "Mm-hmm," in response, hoping it would satisfy.

"Would feel like stealing the food off of her table, you know? Not that I'd watch porn with her in it." Dylan laughed again, oblivious, totally unashamed. "God! Not that you'd think I would. Shit."

"I'd hope not," Rob said. *Please let the roof fall in on our heads.* He rang Dylan through and handed him his change. "Due back next week. Thanks for coming in."

Now please go away.

Thankfully, after pulling his hood back over his head and stuffing the DVD into his front pouch pocket, Dylan did, calling out, "See ya next week!" as he went.

Maybe Rob should trade this shift for one of Max's.

Although God knew how that was supposed to help.

CHAPTER 2

His last night of freedom before the start of winter semester, and Rob wasn't going to waste a single second of it. At eleven-thirty, he locked the front door to Rear Entrance Video, gave the store one last once-over, and stomped up the sidewalk toward the bus stop. At least the rain had stopped.

After giving the wet bench a swipe with his sleeve, he plopped down to wait for his bus and pulled out his cell, which had bleeped with a text.

His sister. *Going out for drinks with some girlfriends, u wanna come?*

Bernice's club of choice was Celebrities, one of Vancouver's venerable old gay bars. Which, naturally, was a scant five or six blocks up from Rear Entrance Video—not that Bernice knew Rob was in the neighbourhood.

Rob hadn't come out to his family, but he had a feeling Bernice knew anyway and was too kind to ask. She was always inviting him out with her girlfriends: shopping, drinks, lunch at the local salad bar, all activities he had to assume were meant to be nonthreatening to his inner gay. Not to mention the yoga.

Or maybe she just knew how badly intimidated he was by other men his age and was hoping girls would be easier. It wasn't like Rob was at all skilled at reading people, even his own sister.

Either way, in the end it didn't really matter. He wasn't sassy or bitchy or well dressed, and yeah, maybe he was a little "obvious," but not in that ideal swishy, theatrical way women seemed to love so much. He was just awkward and mousey and too much of a nerd. Bernice's friends would want to hear his opinions on Ryan Reynolds's godlike abs, and he'd wind up complaining to them about how disappointed he'd been in Reynolds's turn as Deadpool—a wasted opportunity if there ever was one, because Reynolds had been perfect for the part; it was too damn bad about that nightmarishly terrible script.

He thumbed in a quick reply: *Sorry, still busy w/ roommate thing.* Perhaps not strictly true, but hey, maybe when he got home there'd be some Xbox going. At the very least, Austin was good for an all-nighter playing first person shooters (and at least *open* to the possibility of some survival horror) when he wasn't out with his jock buddies.

Bernice's reply was quick in coming: *Boo, you whore. ;)*

Yeah, she definitely knew Rob was gay.

He arrived back at the old house a little under an hour later. The rain had started up again, so he ran the rest of the way home and up the front path with his arms over his head, wishing he hadn't foregone his umbrella. He stood under the leaking porch overhang—God, why was rain dripping from a structure so much colder and grosser than the same rain coming from the sky?—and fumbled with shivering hands through his pockets for his keys. The fucking lock stuck, of course, but at last he got the thing to click and suddenly he was falling through the front door in a pile of wet, teeth-chattering Asian kid.

The house was quiet. Dead silent, actually, the lights low.

Rob poked his head into the living room. The place was . . . Holy shit, immaculate. The throw pillows Christian had insisted on buying were actually *on* the couch. The coffee table was swept free of Doritos residue and takeout containers. No beer bottles scattered around Max's usual spot.

Absurd as it was, Rob felt the weird urge to *creep* through the house. He kicked out of his sneakers, picked them up, and snuck back to the kitchen, which was the only room with a light on. Their Formica kitchen table was draped with a cloth that Rob hadn't even known they had, and topped with a couple of emergency storm candles stuck into wine bottles and two of their only matching plates.

Noah stood at one of the counters, and the rhythmic sound of his quick, precise knifework filled Rob's ears. He felt his body weirdly tighten, not sure why he was responding this way. Well, he knew why: he liked Noah, *liked* liked him to be precise, but even then, watching him cook was an odd thing to fixate on. But then, Rob was an artist, a future sculptor if the universe looked kindly on him. Maybe he just admired seeing that same focus and artistry reflected in another man, even if it was for food instead of clay or stone or paint. Or maybe he just liked the fact that Noah was clearly good with his hands.

The apron cinched tight around his waist and the soft well-worn jeans hugging his ass probably helped too.

Rob cleared his throat, and Noah startled. Turned. He was wearing a button-down shirt underneath his apron.

"Oh, Rob! Hey, buddy," Noah said, still somehow knocked off balance, then shook his head and turned back to his chopping. Onions. A wave of sweet pain hit Rob's eyes the minute he saw them, like some kind of vegetable—or were onions herbs?—placebo effect.

"Hey yourself. Where is everybody?" Rob forced himself to enter the kitchen, fighting that urge to stay back, stay away, avoid imposing himself. Old habits died hard, sure, but Rob had really meant his promise to himself that he wouldn't act that way around his roommates, and really, wasn't six months living with them enough time to get over it? Even so, Rob had horrible visions of himself as the weird kid who never left his room or spoke to anybody, but who paid his rent in full, on time, so nobody could come up with a good enough reason to make him move out.

"Out. I kicked them all out. Austin's crashing at some meathead's, probably drunk off his ass by now, and Max and Christian are at Christian's auntie's until no earlier than 2 a.m."

The way Noah phrased that . . . To Rob, it sounded like Noah had been the one to set that timeline. Reverse-curfew?

"Uh, any particular reason?" Rob asked.

"I'm having a girl over. The hostess from my restaurant, actually. Which I know is a totally stupid idea, but I just can't help myself. Her name's Jenny Chan, her parents are from Hong Kong."

A stab of jealousy hit Rob right in the gut. "Aha. Oh. Um. Do you want me to clear out too?" He could always call Bernice, he supposed. Get changed and pack a bag and show up at Celebrities after all. She'd be pleased.

"Nah, it's cool. I can trust you to keep quiet and out of the way." No question in it, no implied *Can't I?* If there was one thing Rob was very good at, it was keeping to himself.

"Definitely. When's she coming over? What are you making her?"

"Winter squash risotto. Can you believe she's never had risotto before?"

If Austin had been there, he'd have made some borderline racist but toothless comment about Asians and rice, but thank God he wasn't.

"Oh, and she's coming over, um . . ." Noah checked his white plastic watch. "*Shit*, she's supposed to be here—"

The doorbell rang, making its sickly busted up noise that was more like *weee-aung* than *ding-dong*.

"Now?" Rob finished helpfully.

"Shit!" Noah wiped his hands off on the towel he had draped over one shoulder. He nearly fled the room, but then stopped and spun, giving Rob a breathless look. "Do I look okay?"

His hair was messy and sticking up in places, damp with steam from the pan of sautéing squash, his apron spackled with God-knew-what from God-knew-when and God-knew-how-many-washes-ago. And his face was a little flushed.

Yeah. Hot as hell.

"You're good, man. Go."

Noah grinned at him. The doorbell wailed again.

"Go," Rob insisted, half laughing. God, Noah was *nervous*, and there was that jealousy again.

"Oh and, um, Rob?"

"Yes?" God, why was Rob's heart pounding like this?

"You may want to put your headphones on tonight. Just, uh, in case."

Rob wrinkled his nose. He wasn't one of those *Ew, girl parts* kind of guys (or gays, he supposed); he just didn't want to know about Noah's sex life unless that sex life involved him. "Gotcha. Have fun. Be respectful."

Be respectful? Jesus, Rob.

They both walked to the front hall together, Rob taking a turn for the stairwell that took up most of the hall, and Noah heading for the front door. Rob was still on the stairs when Noah finally let Jenny in.

She was beautiful and petite, holding a Burberry-plaid rip-off umbrella, and when she closed it, Rob saw the glitter of a Swarovski hairclip in the shape of a big, girly bow tucked just behind her left ear, sweeping her bangs back. "Hi, Noah. Glad you decided not to leave me on the porch all night," she teased, eyes flicking to Rob and then quickly determining he was of no consequence to her. She beamed at Noah like it was their wedding day, and Rob just knew that Noah was beaming right back.

Jenny Chan, five-foot-something and probably a hundred pounds sopping wet, wearing pink patterned tights underneath her trench coat. Absolutely gorgeous, and, unlike Rob, if *she* was shy then the trait would be as intoxicating as a dab of expensive perfume.

Rob felt that pang of jealousy again. *That could be me.* Not only when it came to dating Noah, but—

No, it couldn't, and we're not going there. Not tonight, not ever.

There was no point in waving good-bye. He was under no social expectation to say, "Nice to meet you," since Noah hadn't introduced them. So he just turned away and carried his wet shoes up the stairs.

Big, noise-cancelling headphones settled over his ears, Rob booted up his Kingdom of Elves account and selected his level-83 dark elf in her comically *un*-protective string bikini armor.

His guild-mates were quick to greet him, their scratchy masculine voices sounding in his ears.

"Hey, sweetie!"

"Evening, cutie!"

He hit the microphone button on his mouse, purring back, "Hi boys, how are you?" Okay, so he did a (surprisingly passable) girl voice over Teamspeak to match his sex-kitten avatar.

So sue him! If he had to choose between the shit he got for being a girl versus the shit he got for being a gay guy, he'd pick the girl anytime. At least the quaint chivalry of dudes hoping for eventual webcam shots or cybersex had its perks. Dubious ones, okay, but perks nonetheless. And maybe this was just his insecurities talking, but he preferred "Sweet Tits" over "Fag-boy" as far as nicknames went, as well.

He picked up some mindless grinding mission: collecting twelve eyeballs off orcs who were apparently mostly blind, considering only one in fifty he killed seemed to drop an eyeball for him to pick up.

Sadly, teen-appropriate cartoon fantasy violence didn't do much for getting his frustrations out. His mind kept straying back to Jenny Chan and Noah downstairs, probably nibbling off each other's forks and trading little giggles and blushes. And Noah would be telling self-deprecating stories about himself to make her laugh, and openly staring at her pretty eyes and pretty smile, which she'd notice but wouldn't say anything about, unless she was the type of person to say something about it, of course . . .

Rob would probably be the type not to point that kind of thing out; instead, he'd just smile more and blush more and bat his eyelashes more, slowly baiting Noah into making a compliment. Or maybe not. Maybe he'd get a coy, mischievous smile instead, and he'd say, *Earth to Noah, did you even hear what I just said?* whether he'd just said something or not. And then Noah would blush back and maybe he'd own up to it—*Sorry for staring, babe, but you're just too beautiful to resist*—or maybe he'd be a little embarrassed at getting caught, and a little flustered, but Rob would soothe his hurt ego by reaching out for his hand and lowering his eyelids and saying, *I didn't tell you that you had to stop.*

"Hey, Bobby," a male voice called in his ear, knocking him out of his Noah fantasy.

"Hi!" Sex-kitten Rob (also known as Bobby) replied. Funny how she sounded so much less mousey than nerdy boy Rob ever could. "How are you doing, Mike?"

Mike was a college student from down in New York, doing some science or another that had him in class all day. And since he seemed to game all night, Rob wasn't exactly sure when the guy slept.

The orc Rob was in the middle of slaying suddenly started taking massive DPS, his hit points withering away, and Mike's muscular Centaur wizard strolled in from one side of Rob's screen. One more hit from Rob's enchanted bow and arrow and the orc fell. Rob tapped the microphone button. "Thanks, babe. I've been at it all damn night."

"I bet you have, you bad girl!" Mike chuckled at the double entendre. "Eyeball quest?"

"You know it."

"How many you have?"

"Like, six?"

"Want some company?"

Rob pulled his legs up under him in his chair and readjusted his headset. "Sure, maybe after we get the last of these, we can get a dungeon group together, run one of your lower-level characters through the Goblin mines?"

"Sounds great. So, hey, uh . . . I've been practicing magic crafting and uh . . . I made this new bow and arrow that boosts your accuracy stats. You want it?"

A trade alert popped up on his screen.

"Holy shit, Mike, that thing's worth two hundred gold. Why don't you sell it?"

"Oh, uh, I was, uh—I was going to sell it, I mean, but I don't really need gold, so I was thinking maybe you . . . I mean if you don't need it, I'll just sell it . . ."

"Mike, be honest, did you specifically make this for me?"

"Are you going to think I'm a total loser if I say yes?"

"Of course I'm not, you goofball." Rob hadn't quite perfected his girl-laugh, so he turned off the mic, as if entirely by accident. Then he accepted the trade.

Dubious perks, indeed.

CHAPTER 3

He and Mike battled orcs for another hour or so after that, until they'd finally collected all twelve of the elusive eyeballs. They collected and then sold the quest's reward, and after that they got a couple of guild-mates and a token gold farmer from Asian countries unknown to run the Goblin mines. Their priest was off his fucking game, though, and Rob joined in on razzing him when their whole party wiped during a minor boss fight.

Of course, then their group's tank had to come in with the fag-this and cocksucker-that, because . . . Well, Rob had no idea where that shit came from, or why it was so fucking ubiquitous. Some sociology or Queer Studies major had probably done a thesis on it, though.

He was about to log off for the night in resignation when Mike came to the rescue, shouting, "There's a lady present! Fucking ingrate."

"Sorry," Casually Homophobic Gamer said, sounding suitably chastened.

"Apology accepted," Rob replied, even though it really, really wasn't.

"Sorry you had to hear that," Mike said, switching over to private chat.

"It's okay, I've heard worse. Thanks for cooling that hothead off for me, though."

"Anything for you, my lady." Man, if Rob weren't a hopeless nerd himself, he'd have laughed at that. Instead, he just felt a pang of affection and commiseration.

He leaned back in his chair, flipping his feet up onto his desk. He'd taken his jeans off before he'd sat down and now his nearly hairless legs were stretched out, glowing, in the flickering light of the computer monitor. He crossed his ankles demurely and dusted at one thigh. "Yeah, well, I think maybe it's a sign I should head to bed, anyway. Got my first day of class tomorrow."

"Oh yeah, definitely don't want to be too tired for the rigorous academic work of your what, basket-weaving degree?"

"BFA in Ceramics, actually."

"Ah yes, my apologies. Millions of old ladies at thousands of farmers' markets are depending on you, then. That's a different matter *entirely*." There was no mistaking the growl in Mike's voice, the way Rob could just *hear* his toothy grin. God, he was *flirting*.

"What about you? Isn't it like 4 a.m. in New York? Gotta be bright-eyed and bushy-tailed for your long day of Bill Nye videos."

And, God, Rob was flirting back.

Mike laughed. "What would I do without you to put me in my place? Gonna miss you tonight, baby."

"Well, I do have to go to bed, but . . ." Might as well. "I don't have to log off just yet . . ."

"Oh, no?" Rob could actually hear Mike swallow through a dry throat.

He was really doing this. Why not? Nobody was home except for Noah, and he'd be way too busy with his own hanky-panky to be worrying about Rob's. And Rob—well, the last couple hours had really invigorated him, made him feel attractive again after a massively shitty day. Maybe Mike was lonely, too. They probably both had their secrets. It didn't have to get any more involved than Rob wanted it to. Being the person you wanted to be, avoiding consequences, forming strange and nebulous connections, wasn't that what the Internet was for?

"Yeah, just give me a second to take off my shirt before I lie down."

"S-sure."

Rob pulled off his headset and stripped away his tee. Put the headset back on and made sure the mic was activated as he lay down. He wanted Mike to hear the mattress creak, hear Rob as he shifted around in his blankets.

"You, uh . . . you sleep shirtless?" Mike was panting a little.

"Mm-hmm. I just get all tangled up in pyjamas, to be honest. So I'm down to my—" he looked down at his plaid boxers "—panties."

"Panties, huh?"

No point in lying more than strictly necessary. "Yeah, they're plaid, from the Gap."

"Wow."

"You don't do this often, do you, Mike?"

"C-can't say I have, no."

Rob could feel his cock shifting and filling, growing fat and tight inside his boxers. He kept his voice sweet. He couldn't let the arousal distract him, although, to be honest, this voice felt more natural than the one he spoke with by light of day. "Aw, that's actually pretty cute to me, actually. Tell me what you're wearing."

"Is this where I tell you some lie? What do girls even like? Is there dude lingerie?"

Rob laughed, but this time it didn't sound masculine at all. "Just tell me the truth."

"Okay, well, you asked for it. I'm wearing tighty-whiteys. You know, like *Breaking Bad*?"

"Sounds sexy. I'll picture that they're Calvin Klein ones instead, okay?"

"Well, I don't look like a Calvin Klein model." Now some insecurity crept into Mike's voice, and Rob's heart went out to him.

"I don't need a Calvin Klein model. I just need a nice, sweet guy who comes to my defense over Teamspeak."

"Heh, well that I can do." Confidence returned. "So what do *you* look like?"

"Well, I'm Asian, so I'm pretty small and have black hair."

"Yeah?"

Rob looked down at his body, and the sight strangely didn't bother him at all. There was no dissonance, even though Mike was probably picturing Lucy Liu or Zhang Ziyi. In the dim computer light, Rob could picture the slightest curve to his slim hips, and his legs were delicate and pretty. His cock, well, he'd never minded that.

"I'm, uh . . . well, half German, part Irish, maybe some Scottish in there." *So, white, then.* Rob couldn't help but smile to himself at that. "Little bit chubby."

"I like that."

"Yeah?"

"Yeah, I bet I'd feel so small in your arms. I bet my face would fit perfectly against your chest. Do you have a hairy chest, Mike?" Rob said his name like he was calling up a god for a spell.

"Yeah."

"Mmm, can I scratch my fingernails through it?" Rob's hand skimmed down his flat belly and disappeared under the waistband of his boxers. He scratched his fingers through his neat pubic hair, pretending it was the blond half-German hair that formed a sexy triangle between Mike's part-Irish pink nipples.

"Yeah . . ." Mike replied, breathing a little hard.

"Are you touching yourself, Mike?"

Mike barked out a little laugh. "How could I not?"

"How about you let me do that instead? Are you cut or uncut, Mike?" Rob wrapped a hand around his own (cut) cock and gave himself a slow jerk.

"*Ungh*, I'm cut."

"Mmm, nice. I bet you have a nice head that I could lick and suck on."

"God, *fuck*."

Rob fumbled to one side and found his bedside drawer, yanking it open and quickly finding his lube. He overslicked his hand, kicking out of his boxers. He ran his wet fingers between his legs and up his crack, homing in on his hungry hole. He wished Mike were here, that Mike would turn him over and fuck his ass but call it a pussy. "Getting so wet for you, baby. You mind if I finger myself while I suck your big dick?"

"Go ahead. Please. Are you . . . are you tight? Down there?" Finally getting up the nerve to join in, even if his effort wasn't terribly inspiring.

"*Down there?*" Rob chuckled. "You mean my pussy, Mike? Is my pussy tight?"

"Yeah," Mike groaned back.

"It's *so* tight, Mike. I'm no virgin, but your dick wouldn't be able to tell."

Mike's breath hitched.

"I'm putting a finger in my pussy now, Mike. Gonna suck your dick. Might be a little too big for me though. You going to make me take it? Make me choke on your dick?"

"Only if you want to. I'm a gentleman."

"Mmm, good answer," Rob praised, then shoved a single finger into his hole. His *pussy*, fuck. He fell into the familiar gender-bending fantasy, raising his free hand to his mouth, shoving three fingers in, and licking them up and down, making it wet and loud for Mike to hear. Pressed back with them until he gagged.

"God, God," Mike babbled back, and his breaths were coming hard and fast now. Rob imagined that those harsh breaths were from fucking so hard, from grabbing Rob's hips and pounding his pussy, tearing into him with that raw cut dick. "Can I touch your tits?"

Rob pulled his spit-wet hand out of his mouth and started pumping his aching, hard dick with it, glad he had the dexterity to jerk off and finger-fuck himself at the same time. "I'd prefer if you sucked on them, Mike. Get my nipples hard, maybe bite me a little?"

"You like that?"

"Oh, yes," Rob murmured, adding another finger, and then another, three fingers stretching his wet pussy wide. The tip of his middle one grazed his prostate and he arched off his bed with a cry.

"I'm holding both of your tits in my hands now, rubbing them a little."

"Squeeze them."

"They're so soft."

"Yeah, small but mighty."

"Su-sucking your nipples now," Mike said. "Oh, oh!"

"About to come?" Rob asked. He sure as hell was.

"Fuck, sorry, yeah, close, I'm close—"

"It's okay, baby. Come on my tits. Give me a pearl necklace to wear."

"Yes, yes, God. You're so hot, Bobby, so hot, so hot—"

Mike's voice devolved into grunts and moans at the same time Rob clenched hard on his fingers and shot right up his stomach and chest.

They lay together awhile after that, across the continent but together, both panting and humming as their bodies twitched and came to rest.

At last, Rob grabbed his balled-up dirty boxers and wiped his stomach and chest clean.

"That was great," Mike said, finally recovering himself.

"Yeah. Just one thing before you go."

"Anything, baby."

Rob took a deep breath and closed his eyes, because now the shame was hitting him hard. "I did this because I like you and you're a good guy, not because you gave me loot, right?"

"Not a prostitute. Gotcha."

"*Virtual* prostitute," Rob corrected with a dopey smile.

Mike's voice was soft and kind. "Sweet dreams, baby."

"Sweet dreams." Rob turned off his mic, stretched to turn his computer monitor off, pulled the headset from his head, and finally, *finally*, rolled over to sleep.

CHAPTER 4

When Rob came downstairs the next morning, Christian was already in the kitchen, chewing on some toast as he looked over his imposing binder of lesson plans.

"Coffee?" Rob asked hopefully, and Christian nodded his head toward the pot on the counter.

"Made enough for both of us," Christian replied, not looking up.

"Thanks, you're a gentleman."

Mike's voice, echoing in Rob's head: *I'm a gentleman.*

The phrase gave Rob a weird surge of mixed humiliation/pleasure that he quickly shoved down again. There was no room for Bobby by the light of day.

"I know," Christian said with a smile, and took a sip from his own mug.

Rob dropped a couple of slices of rye into the toaster, then poured himself a coffee in his usual mug. Went to the fridge for milk while his bread toasted.

He and Christian had fallen into something of a routine, as the only ones up early. Austin either had afternoon classes or *early*—as in, 5 a.m. early—morning hockey practice, and Max and Noah were both night owls who slept in until at least noon whenever they could. Christian and Rob, however, both had strict schedules and were strict enough with *themselves* to keep them.

"When did you get in last night?" Rob asked.

"Two-ish." Christian didn't actually say, *Just as I was told to*, but Rob could feel it dangling off the end, there. "You? How was your shift?"

"Went good. Charlie VIP came in."

"Didn't let him kiss you, did you?"

Rob laughed a little, thinking of Charlie's scabby mouth. Poor perverted bastard, although considering what had gone down between Rob and Mike last night, maybe Charlie was in good company. "Nah. So, uh . . . was what's-her-name—" Her name was Jenny, of course, but Rob didn't quite want to admit to remembering it as well as he did. "Um, you know, was she still here when you got back?"

"Unless you've taken to wearing ballet flats recently, I think so."

"Still here now?"

"Jesus, Rob, I don't know, I didn't go check the front hall before I took my morning piss. Why do you care?"

Rob blushed furiously and turned to butter his toast, which he did a little more angrily than was strictly necessary. "I don't!" The soft bread tore under the cold margarine.

"Oookay. Well, I don't know. Maybe she did, maybe she didn't. As long as she pays rent if she makes a long-term habit of it, I really don't care."

"Do you think Noah would go for that?" Rob may not have been too hot on the idea of Noah shacking up with someone who wasn't Rob himself, but even he couldn't resist the thought of a break on his rent. Sure, his parents footed the bill, but that didn't mean Rob couldn't still be frugal on their behalf—after all, if money was no object, then he could have lived somewhere way nicer than here.

"He'd better, considering Max and I are both paying the exact same rent we were before we hooked up, even though now we're sharing a room."

"Yeah, well, don't get ahead of yourself. Sharing a *bed*, sure, but don't tell me Max has moved anything but the essentials out of his old room. There's no way we could turn around and rent that tomorrow, if we wanted to."

"Hmmph," Christian sniffed, but there was no mistaking the look of acquiescence on his face. "Yeah, well, if Noah *wanted* to rent out the room, we could clean it. Well, I could clean it and Max could supervise."

"Supervise. Right." Rob chuckled through a mouthful of toast. "Anyway, I don't think Noah's gonna be renting that room out any time soon. I'm not sure what the occupancy density threshold is for this place to qualify as slum housing."

Christian reached for the nearest wall, flaking off some ancient yellow paint with his fingernails. "You telling me it's *not* slum housing already?"

"It has *character*," Rob countered.

"Uh-huh. I believe that's what your ad said."

"Yeah, well, at this price point I think those kinds of cosmetic nuances fall under that banner."

"Man, forget pottery or sculpture or whatever, you should go into advertising."

Rob gave an exaggerated dreamy sigh. "Oh yes, using T and A to sell sneakers to impressionable kids who can't afford them."

Christian thought it over a moment, then came back with, "Vodka to alcoholics."

"Las Vegas vacations to gambling addicts."

"Barbie dolls to the parents of gender-rebelling little girls."

Rob scrunched up his nose. "Better not."

"Better not," Christian agreed.

A brisk wind came in from False Creek, and Rob yanked his scarf around his nose as he walked. A shivering busker on the street corner playing a fiddle with wind-chapped hands gave him a nod and a smile as he passed, and Rob nodded back with a pitying look, but didn't stop. If he gave change to every busker he encountered on his twice-daily walk across Granville Island on the way to and from school, he'd bankrupt his parents by the time he finally graduated. One day when he was rich and famous from his art—*ha!*—perhaps he'd spare them more. Or maybe he'd put aside a fund from his Rear Entrance Video earnings to be distributed over the course of a month to the musicians and performers who really *spoke* to him.

Yes, that.

His guilt soothed, he hurried down the not-sidewalk and through the maze of former industrial buildings to the looming repurposed factory he'd been calling school since September.

At this time of the morning the island was quiet, just the sounds of trucks unloading produce and goods, the tinkle of coffee shop doors, the murmur of sleepy art students like himself, and the piercing cries of gulls. Even in the off-season, by late afternoon this place would be bustling with tourists and locals, here to window-shop, sample beer and wine, and pretend they understood the art. And only *rarely* buy anything, if the dissatisfied grumblings of his fellow students were to be believed.

He joined the usual throng of girls in colored tights and guys in skinny jeans bottle-necked at the main entrance to the North building. Once he was safely inside and could feel his hands again, he pulled out his class schedule and squinted at it. Mondays and Wednesdays both started with two hours of *Introduction to Art Principles* in a classroom space, followed by an hour for lunch, and then three hours of studio time. Rob wasn't really drooling at the thought of going over stuff like negative space with a bunch of fellow first-years here for everything from oil painting and animation through to photography and . . . well, *basket weaving*. None of whom wanted to be in this lame first-year class, either, but they were all stuck with it anyway.

At least it wasn't *Introduction to Art History*.

After working up the nerve to ask someone who looked suitably older and more worldly than he was for directions to his class, he was off. The "lecture hall," such as it was, was nothing like the huge auditoriums he'd toured at SFU and UBC during high school: it was a small, cramped classroom lined on all walls by shelves and counters covered in half-finished art, and wedged in the center of it all was a cluster of tables and chairs and a projector.

Rob selected a seat close to the projector—this was college, he was *so* over pretending not to be a keener—and began to go through his bag. Pen. Pencils. Notepads, lined and unlined.

All around him, his fellow students sat in small clusters, trading gossip over the Starbucks they'd carried over from the "mainland." Three white girls, all in a near uniform of cardigans, floaty patterned dresses, and knee-high boots. Two Asian girls with edgy razored haircuts, one of them with a bright pink streak in her bangs, both speaking Mandarin. A mixed group of five made up of all different races and genders but who had apparently found common ground in their taste for thick-rimmed glasses. Two middle-aged women, both in hand-knit clothes. Rob vaguely recognized a couple of his classmates from last semester, but most were new faces—not that it made a difference, seeing as he hadn't exchanged more than two words with any of them. He watched the seats fill with more people, everyone with friends or in the process of making them.

At two minutes to the start of class, one straggler came through the door, a big guy wearing a sweatshirt, the hood pulled up over his head.

Oh crap.

It was ERASE RACISM guy. From the store. What was his name, again? Darryl? Dennis? *Dylan.*

Dylan's eyes landed on Rob, briefly, then glanced away, not a spark of recognition in them, thank God. Not that Rob was ashamed of working at a porn store, but that didn't mean he wanted to cross the streams, so to speak, and especially not with a chatterbox like Dylan.

Dylan found a seat near the back and fell into it, quickly making himself comfortable with his skater-sneakered feet on his desk and his big binder open on his lap. He kept his hood up. He didn't talk to *anyone*. In fact, he seemed downright mean. Unapproachable. Nothing like the person Rob had suffered so much talking to at Rear Entrance Video, where he'd been obnoxious, but in a very friendly and maybe even charming way.

Oh well, not Rob's problem. He faced front, focusing on the blank pull-down screen until the professor came in.

She seemed pretty disorganized, dropping pens and fumbling through transparencies, then spending five minutes flicking the projector's on/off switch uselessly until one of the girls in the cardigan crew pointed out that it wasn't plugged in.

Once the projector was lit up and humming, she uncapped a pen and scrawled something on the projector's surface, which appeared on the screen behind her as a purple blob. Another several agonizing minutes spent adjusting the focus knob, and finally her name came into view.

Doctor Chastity Sylvain.

"But you can call me Doctor Chastity," she said with a smile, and somebody snorted.

Someone from the back of the room.

"And your name is?" Doctor Chastity asked with a slightly tense smile.

Rob didn't have to look to know who she was talking to.

"Dylan, ma'am. Doctor Chastity, ma'am." Before she had to ask the question written all over her face—*And what is so funny here, Dylan?*—he offered up, "Sorry for laughing, ma'am, it's just that 'Doctor Chastity' sounds like a sexy Bond villain."

Doctor Chastity surprised Rob by laughing. "Or a dominatrix, but I guess Bond villain's more PG."

"You said it," Dylan joked back, and this time they both laughed. Maybe he was still nice, after all.

"Since it's the first day of a new semester, I thought we'd start by going around the room and introducing ourselves—" Doctor Chastity rolled her eyes at the class's mass groan. "—and then go over the syllabus, which should take us to around the halfway point of class, after which I'll be glad to *dismiss you early*." No mistaking the reasoning for the emphasis on the last bit, there: their chances of an early dismissal entirely depended on how well they played along with everything that came before, namely the going-around-the-room-and-sharing part, Rob had to assume. "So how about we start with you, Dylan?"

"You're just pickin' on me because you know my name," Dylan protested.

"Yes, and?"

"And nothin', just wanted to point out I was onto you. Anyway, my name's—"

"Stand up and introduce yourself," Doctor Chastity corrected.

Dylan grumbled and tossed his binder onto the desk, seeming to purposely make the act of standing up one of the most difficult things a human body could do, like a fucking Olympic event. "This is against my human rights, you know."

Doctor Chastity rolled her eyes at him.

"Okay. Now that I'm *standing*, my name's Dylan. I'm twenty-three, majoring in illustration, which is a fancy way of saying I draw comics." He paused for effect, then sniffed in disgust and added, "None of that big-eyed anime shit, though."

Huh, Rob was beginning to like the art-school version of Dylan.

"I was born in Nunavut, and yeah, I'm Inuit, but I got white parents, and I don't do no soapstone carving shit."

"Thank you, Dylan," Doctor Chastity said. *But that will be enough.*

"You're welcome," Dylan replied, deadpan, and sat.

One of the middle-aged women went next, adjusting the drape of her shawl as she stood. "I'm Theresa, I've been twenty-nine for fifteen years—" A polite chuckle from those seated closest to her. "—and I'm majoring in fine arts, watercolors mostly, but only because they don't formally have a textile arts program here."

"We do have a very popular spinning and weaving club," Doctor Chastity said.

"Oh, I'm already the treasurer of that."

Doctor Chastity nodded to herself, arms crossed. "Of course you are."

After Theresa had extolled the virtues of knitting a bit more, Doctor Chastity finally waved her back into her seat so that the next person—one of the matching-glasses crew—could stand and start his own monologue, which was a rambling diatribe about why he thought art school was a crock of shit, but if he didn't attend, his mother would be cutting him off.

One by one, they went through the class. Like any first-year breadth requirement course, there was your requisite mix of students from all different programs and specializations. Other than Dylan, who had a weird, crass magnetism to him that Rob couldn't ignore, Rob daydreamed for five minutes to every one minute he spent actively listening.

Of course, by "actively listening," he mostly meant straining to see whether it was or would soon be his turn to speak.

And by "daydreaming," he mostly meant thinking about Dylan.

Why did he have white parents? Why had he travelled so far? What kind of comics *did* he draw? Why was he so edgy about soapstone carving? Did he recognize Rob from the store? Would they become friends? Or maybe enemies, because Rob knew too much? Would Dylan ignore him and hope Rob did the same, keeping his two lives separate?

Well, if anything did happen between them, Rob would let Dylan make the first move, whether that meant extending a hand in friendship or extending a fist in punching. And then, because one of the cardigan girls seemed to be telling her entire fucking life story,

Rob spent a few minutes entertaining the thought that it all might just be a case of mistaken identities, that the Dylan of art class and the Dylan of Rear Entrance Video were two separate Dylans.

And since that theory was patently fucking ridiculous, that just left two-point-five possibilities: Rob was forgettable, just one Chinese kid in a Hongcouver half-million; or that Dylan recognized Rob but was purposely choosing not to acknowledge him for one reason or another. Which left . . . Was that a bad thing? Rob wasn't sure. He should probably accept it as a good thing. He should be relieved that Dylan actually had some discretion, and whether that was born out of more tact that Rob had originally attributed to him or out of shame, well, that wasn't Rob's fucking problem, was it?

So why did he feel so . . . Shitty? Overlooked? Unremarkable?

Bobby.

If Dylan had walked into that store last night and Bobby had been the one sitting behind the counter, if Rob really *was* Bobby, in the real world and not just the lame-o fantasy elf one, would today have gone differently? Would Dylan have recognized him? Would Dylan have acknowledged him, sat beside him, struck up a conversation?

Her, dammit.

Bobby was a she, and Rob was a he, and by the light of day never the twain would meet. Whatever little fantasies Rob had about alternate realities, in this world, men were men and women were women, whether you were born that way or you had a sex-change or whatever, that part didn't matter. What mattered was that you couldn't be *both*.

He sighed miserably and pillowed his head in his hands. The girl with the pink streak was speaking now, something about repurposed industrial material reformed into disturbing and thought-provoking sculptural pieces, but Rob couldn't bring himself to care.

He couldn't bring himself to care about any of them. He didn't bother trying to remember their names, even though his resolution had been to make friends and be more social. And how in the hell was he going to do that if he didn't even know people's names and programs as a jumping-off point? How would he ever become the person he wanted to be if all he did was lie around moping about a person he *couldn't* be?

Next week, he decided. Next week he'd come in and sit next to someone and introduce himself.

Doctor Chastity's somewhat bored and annoyed voice broke through his thoughts. "And you? Excuse me? Are you asleep? Is he asleep? Can somebody poke that kid?"

Or he could introduce himself right now, because that's what they'd been doing before he'd taken a one-way train to Self-pityville.

He sat up quickly. "No need to poke me. Sorry, uh, I work nights." He cast a careful glance over in Dylan's direction, but no look of recognition appeared on his face, even with the hint. In fact, Dylan looked a little like he was sleeping sitting up with his eyes open. Well, good. Let the guy sleep the whole way through Rob's introduction, and maybe he'd *never* make the Rear Entrance Video connection.

That settled, Rob stood and cleared his throat. Picked at a spontaneously loose thread on the sleeve of his tee. "I'm Rob Ng. That's N-G pronounced like I-N-G. Ng. I'm nineteen—" *crushing on my straight male roommate who won't so much as glance at me* "—in first year, just graduated high school." *And I wish I was a girl.* "I'm hoping to go into ceramics, but I love sculpture in all its forms." And then, because he was some kind of masochist and maybe he really *did* want Dylan to notice him, whether he wound up recognizing him or not, finished, "Even soapstone carving."

No reaction. Not from Dylan, not from anybody.

And goddamn if Rob couldn't help but think that if it had been Bobby telling that joke, they'd have all—Dylan included—been in fucking stitches.

Rob drummed out a distracted rhythm on the counter with his highlighter, eyes slipping half focused from the pages of his textbook to the watch on his wrist and back again. One more hour until the store closed, ten more pages to read, and good God, was it really only his first day of this? He sighed, groaned, read two lines of the exact same paragraph he'd been trying to read this entire shift, then slammed the textbook closed. Maybe he'd have better luck on the bus home tonight. Or the bus to school tomorrow morning. Or not at all.

Capping his highlighter, he cast a glance around the store, looking for any task to keep his hands busy. He felt weirdly anxious, like he was right on the edge of something important, some change or transformation or decision . . . or maybe he just needed to get a new prescription for Zoloft.

But the shelves were all neatly stacked, the returns all put away, the toys all dusted, and even the peepshow booths were acceptable enough that he didn't feel guilty not cleaning them, and he sure as hell wasn't antsy to the point of raising his standards there. In fact, he wasn't sure he *could* get to that point; he didn't even like his own cum, let alone someone else's, let alone someone like Charlie VIP's.

With nothing else to do, he was just about to start counting out the till early when the doorbell chimed.

Customers. Of course. Two college-aged guys, one in a UBC hoodie and the other in a Hollister ball cap. Drunk, judging by the way they were swerving.

Well, at least it wasn't Charlie VIP . . . or Dylan. Rob wasn't sure he could get away with not being recognized more than once.

"I *cannot* believe we met Chichi Yamaguchi," Hollister Cap said, leading the charge toward the Asian Fetish section.

"Yeah, well, *I* can't believe you seriously got her to sign your abs," his buddy replied, to which Hollister Cap stopped and pulled up his shirt, revealing a chiseled stomach with a black Sharpie scrawl.

"I'm never going to wash this stomach again," he said before dropping his shirt. The two of them disappeared behind a tall shelf, their loud drunken voices still carrying to Rob's ears.

"Gross, dude. Not even after practice?"

"Not even after practice."

"Well, whatever, you enjoy your life not showering. Me, I'm gonna make her my wife."

"You gonna marry a porn star? Dude, naw."

"That's why they call it making an honest woman of her."

"Uh-huh, uh-huh. Only honesty you're gonna get is when she tells you she gave you the clap."

"Chichi Yamaguchi is an unspoiled Chinese flower."

"Chichi Yamaguchi is Japanese."

"Chinese."

"Japanese."

They went on like that for way too long, until Rob had to sit on his hands to keep himself from sticking his fingers in his ears. That kind of thing probably wouldn't be considered good customer service if they caught him at it.

"Well, whatever she is, she's fine as hell. Tiny little titties."

"Not enough girls in porn brave enough to say no to fake tits."

"Chinese girls don't fuckin' get fake tits."

"Japanese."

"Do you think it's weird to rent a video with her after we just met her?"

"I wanna jerk it with the hand that shook her hand."

"No fuckin' way you're jerking off in front of me, man. That's gay."

"So you're saying that if Chichi Yamaguchi was here right now and asked us for a threesome, that would be gay? Even if she was sucking you off and I was fucking her, Chinese fingercuffs style?"

"Japanese."

"Whatever, man. You think that would be gay?"

"Long as you don't stare into my eyes the whole time."

"So how's that different from jerking off to porn of her?"

"Okay, but I better not catch you looking at my junk."

"Yeah, I'm gonna have Chichi fuckin' Yamaguchi getting it up the ass in front of me and I'm gonna be looking at *your* dick."

"Told you you were a fag."

"Bend over and I'll show you how much of a fag I am."

"Sick, dude!" said the guy in the UBC sweatshirt as they rounded the shelves again, and Rob quickly schooled his face into neutral blankness, like he hadn't heard a word of their ridiculous conversation. *Homophobic. Racist. Asinine.*

Hollister Cap dropped the DVD case on the counter. Chichi Yamaguchi winked up at Rob through her circle lenses and fake eyelashes, cupping her breasts in both hands with a Photoshop-enhanced pink blush. "Hey little man, quit drooling and do the rental. Get your own DVD."

"WE WANT TO RENT DVD. DVD. RENT," UBC Sweatshirt added, using expansive hand gestures for emphasis, then looked to Hollister Cap for approval. They both laughed.

Ah yes, pretending Rob didn't speak English. The height of comedy. Rob forced himself not to roll his eyes. "Yes. I just need your membership card." A couple of years ago, when he'd been younger and meeker and more self-loathing, he'd have tried to tell them he spoke English just fine and had been born here, and he would say it all with a carefully rehearsed Canadian accent, no trace of his parents in it. Now he was through giving a shit. These guys didn't deserve an apology, and they didn't need an explanation. They weren't ignorant (in the traditional sense of the word, at least), they were just fucking assholes.

"What, you need a card? What the fuck kind of place you running here?" UBC Sweatshirt spat.

"A normal video rental place?" Rob asked, not sure what else he was supposed to say.

"Man, that's bullshit, I don't want to tell you who I am. Shit, why does anyone even come here anyway when they got the whole internet?"

"The personal service?" Rob muttered to himself, and then his eyes bugged out. He hadn't meant to say that. *Oh God, abort, abort, abort, do not engage meatheads.*

"The fuck? Are you coming on to us?"

"What was that, porn guy? You wanna give us some 'personal service?'"

Sigh.

"C'mon man, let's get the fuck out of this sketch shop and watch her on JerkTube instead." UBC slapped his cap-wearing compatriot on the back in a show of meathead solidarity, and they stormed away together, extending matching middle fingers at Rob just before they slipped out the door and it slammed shut behind them.

With a sigh of misery-slash-relief, Rob put his face in his hands.

Through his fingers, Chichi Yamaguchi—looking cute and airbrushed with some gibberish neon kanji blocking out her pussy—seemed to taunt him. How come she got treated like some kind of goddess while Rob was just some coolie piece of shit?

Those two meatheads wouldn't have treated Bobby that way.

Shit.

CHAPTER 5

Rob wasn't exactly sure *why* he'd rented the Chichi Yamaguchi video, but there it was, lying on his bed, half spilled out of his backpack with his textbooks and pencils. He thought maybe he would ignore it at first, bring it back to the store tomorrow, unwatched, and chalk it up to some kind of lapse in judgment, but it didn't take long for him to give in to temptation.

Well, it wasn't temptation, exactly; temptation implied that it was something he desired and craved, like chocolate or Long Island Iced Tea. More like compulsion, because even though he didn't want to watch the video, would gain no pleasure from it, he just *had* to. Had to see her for himself and really know where the lines between her and him were drawn.

Just what the fuck was so special about her, huh?

God, between this and the multiple I-wish-I-was-really-Bobby moments today, Rob was headed straight off the deep end. Oh well, might as well jump in feet first.

He shucked out of his jeans, put on his headphones, dropped the disc into his computer's CD-ROM drive, and sat back in his chair.

The video the meatheads had selected was called *Kawaii Cuties,* and Rob wasn't actually sure what to expect. He didn't know if it was some repackaged import with spliced-together scenes from various not-too-rapey Japanese pornos, the kind with no English dialogue and pixelated genitals, or if it was just your average domestic yellow-fever vid with Asian American actresses playing up their Asianness probably for the first and only time in a life spent insisting that despite their race, they belonged here.

Kawaii Cuties wound up being an American production, with Chichi Yamaguchi headlining a mixed, thoroughly American cast.

Not that Rob could tell the specific ancestry of the women without some kind of context cues, but at the very least he was pretty sure a few were first-generation Filipina American, by their accents.

Before every actress's scene, the director interviewed them sitting on a big red armchair in a featureless room, half naked. He asked them dumb and humiliating questions about whether their parents knew about their porn careers, how old they were, what their cutest feature was, did they like it up the ass . . . Rob stopped listening about three minutes in, waiting until the part when Chichi Yamaguchi took the screen. Eventually, equal parts bored and disgusted, he started skipping scenes: blowjob, blowjob, a new interview, money shot, gynaecological straight shot of dick in pussy, another interview, two women tongue-kissing, and then, at last, Rob hit play when he spotted Chichi Yamaguchi in her Elegant Gothic Lolita getup of ruffly, pink babydoll dress and white Mary Jane platform shoes. She spent her time in the red armchair giggling behind her hand, often shying away from giving direct answers to his questions, pleading bad English or blushing and clutching her cheeks and whimpering "Nooooo!" like she was playing backup for Gwen Fucking Stefani.

You'd have to be a serious sicko to get off on this kind of thing, especially when the director told her to take off her dress and Chichi yelped "I'm shy!" before jumping right to it anyway. Which was why it was seriously fucked-up that Rob had a boner right now.

He felt himself sinking into Chichi's skin, her perfectly coiffed hair falling over his cheeks, her embellished, glittery nails tracing sharp shallow paths up his inner thighs as he touched himself. On screen in front of him, they'd moved past the ridiculous interview portion of proceedings. Two big, tanned white guys entered the picture, already naked and rock hard. One from each side of the frame, and Chichi greeted them both with titters, especially as their cocks nudged her cheeks. Just like with taking off her dress, though, that gauzy curtain of embarrassment and shyness and hesitation was quickly and easily pulled aside, revealing the enthusiastic professional underneath.

Why the act?

Rob didn't get it, but then, he wasn't terribly motivated to analyze beyond the surface, especially not now that Chichi had a cock in each long-nailed hand, jerking off one meathead while she sucked on the fat purple knob of the other. Rob pictured himself squatting like that—in all the position's incongruously graceful glory—naked except for his heels, legs spread obscenely and erection pointing straight at the camera. And on either side of him, the two meatheads from Rear Entrance Video, their hands in his hair and their cocks fighting for space in his wet, desperate mouth. They may have overlooked the mousey boy behind the counter at the porn store, but here in his fantasy they were completely at his beck and call, helpless in the face of his sexual glamour.

They begged for his body. He deigned to let them have it.

Broken, masculine moans filled his ears and saliva filled his mouth as he closed his eyes and pictured the bittersalt taste of those cocks, imagined sucking one off while the other rubbed up the crack of his ass, up and down, a thick bruiser of a prick parting his cleft, threatening to claim his tight, tempting pussy.

In his fantasy, he didn't need to lubricate himself. He was wet and ready, like the girl he was. That big dick slipped into him easy-as-you-please, nudging right past his clenching muscles and filling every inch of him.

In the real world, he wrapped his hand around his cock, jerking himself dry with a rough, artless hand, picturing it was that meathead's hand, the hand of a man desperate to touch him but too hungry to be as gentle and worshipful as Bobby deserved. That was all right. Bobby liked it rough, just so long as the guy's heart was in the right place.

"Yes," he moaned softly to himself as Chichi cried out in his ears. She'd probably faked her orgasm.

Bobby didn't.

Rob was still gasping and shivering, Chichi Yamaguchi's O-face paused on his monitor and one hand still drenched in sticky cum, when a chat window popped up on screen.

He blinked a couple times, trying to focus the blur of his post-orgasm vision. The text swam in front of his eyes a couple seconds more, and then something in his brain kicked into gear and the words sharpened into legibility.

LetsDoScience: Hey cutie, missed you today!
LetsDoScience: You in for the raid Friday night?
LetsDoScience: Hello?
LetsDoScience: You there?

Mike! Shit! The guy had some kind of uncanny Bobby-sex radar.

Rob fell half off his chair, scrabbling for a piece of laundry dirty enough that he wouldn't feel bad about getting cum all over it. At last, he caught a balled-up sock between his fingers, managed to grab hold of it, and righted himself again.

By the time he'd gotten his hand cleaned off, several more messages had appeared.

LetsDoScience: Are you mad at me?
LetsDoScience: Is it about the other night??
LetsDoScience: Look if you're embarrassed about the other night forget it, I won't bring it up if you don't want.
LetsDoScience: Please?

Jeez, being a girl was a full-time job, wasn't it?

Even if Rob was only one part-time.

He took a deep breath, realizing the delay was less about "channeling Bobby" and more about making sure he didn't say the wrong thing to Mike. Bobby just came naturally, it seemed.

FakeGeekGirl93: OMG sorry Mike!
FakeGeekGirl93: I was AFK, forgot to put up away message
FakeGeekGirl93: sorry sorry
FakeGeekGirl93: I'm not embarrassed about the other night at all, why would I be embarrassed?
LetsDoScience: Oh LOL. Sorry for freaking out, I was just worried I scared you off or something.
FakeGeekGirl93: No! Never, LOL. ;)
LetsDoScience: Well in that case, webcam?
FakeGeekGirl93: ???
LetsDoScience: No funny stuff! Just want to see your pretty face, if that's okay?
FakeGeekGirl93: Yeah right no funny stuff u horndog.
LetsDoScience: Cross my heart. I'm not a "tits or gtfo" kinda guy.
FakeGeekGirl93: Thank god for that.
FakeGeekGirl93: I don't put out for /b/tards.

LetsDoScience: Sound policy.
LetsDoScience: So... cam? Please?
FakeGeekGirl93: OMG I just got out of the shower. No makeup.
Raincheque?
LetsDoScience: Friday after the raid?

Okay, Rob had just been intending to put it off again and again until Mike eventually got the hint and gave up asking, maybe even gave up talking to him all together. So actually setting a date was a whole other level.

He opened his webcam without connecting to Mike and stared at his face reflected in the monitor, the shadowy moving image overlapping the still, brightly lit one of Chichi Yamaguchi on pause.

LetsDoScience: Hello?
LetsDoScience: AFK again?
LetsDoScience: You can say no if you want.

Rob tilted his chin down. Turned his face to the left a little. Changed the angle of the webcam's camera. Ruffled his hair with his fingers so that his bangs hung in his eyes a little. Bit his lip and smiled at himself. Leaned forward, squeezed his chest with his upper arms until a light shadow cut down between his pecs.

FakeGeekGirl93: This Friday?
FakeGeekGirl93: What the hell, why not?
FakeGeekGirl93: Ok let's do it.
LetsDoScience: Yay!!!
FakeGeekGirl93: Friday after the raid. It's a date ;)

The rest of Rob's week passed in a frantic blur of *What the hell was I thinking?*

In classes he mostly kept to himself, occasionally sneaking glances at Dylan as they passed one another in the halls, but never letting his gaping transform into anything . . . less creepy. Or sad. Creepy *and* sad? Whatever.

Whenever Rob saw him, Dylan seemed to be alone. Alone at the lunch counter. Alone waiting for the bus. Alone in studio with big headphones over his ears. On Wednesday, when they had more *Introduction to Art Principles*, he shot the shit with Doctor Chastity, but otherwise? Yeah, alone. The other students in their cliques seemed to give him a wide berth.

Rob, they just flat-out ignored, and Rob found himself spending more time than was healthy trying to decide which was worse. All the well-intentioned resolutions in the world (make friends, stop being such a loser, make eye contact with people, learn to live IRL) couldn't breed the neurosis out of him, apparently, so he just stopped trying. Latched onto his hopes for Bobby, instead.

Although God knew why he thought of that as a viable alternative. What was he going to do, make a midsemester transition and hope nobody remembered he'd spent the first few weeks—not to mention his entire first semester—as a guy? Or that he'd existed at all?

Now that was a nice thought. Clean slate. Walk into the class, introduce himself as Bobby Ng, and he'd just be the new girl, and that status would inspire friendliness in his classmates. They'd introduce themselves, ask him to sit with their friends, invite him to lunch.

They'd invite him to lunch, but he'd say no, and ask Dylan instead.

For like a pizza or something, okay? Not *out* out. Not on a date, just lunch with a classmate where they could complain about their assignments and Dylan's taste in porn. No, scratch that. He couldn't get close to Dylan, because the closer he got, the more likely it would be that Dylan would make the connection.

Not that Rob cared if Dylan knew he worked in a porn store, right? No way. He just didn't want to have any awkward conversations in public places.

Yeah, wouldn't want his classmates thinking he was *weird*, now would he?

He didn't even know anymore what he was afraid of, what he wanted.

Because really, say he *could* show up as the new girl Bobby Ng, would that make him happy? Once he made the switch, he'd have to stick to it, and he wasn't sure he was actually all that interested in committing to a new gender identity. After all, if he was really dedicated to the whole girl thing, he'd have picked a girl name that wasn't still mostly a boy's name and—oh, by the way, just a nickname for the one-hundred-percent boy name that his parents had given him.

And that was assuming that if he walked in dressed up as Bobby, he'd even pass for a real girl. He did online, as far as he knew, but IRL his only cross-dressing experience had been last Halloween when he'd gone in drag to *Rocky Horror*, and he hadn't been *trying* to pass then.

Although other than his guy voice, he was pretty sure he had.

Passed, that was. On first glance, at least.

Which was amazing.

Rob was a pretty slightly built guy, but he still had facial hair and an Adam's apple and no boobs and a naturally deeper voice and, and, and. And sure, those things could be corrected if you took hormones and went to speech therapy or had surgery, but Rob didn't want to do any of those things. And even if those measures were completely painless (which they weren't) and nonpermanent (were they?), he didn't *want* to change his body. It was inconvenient, sure, but it was his.

So even if they did forget Rob existed, would they even buy the premise of Bobby? Somebody would be able to tell, especially since Rob wasn't all that keen on drastic changes. One slipup and it would be nothing but silent judgment and intrusive questions about his genitals... Not to mention, y'know, *bigotry*. Rob was sheltered, but he wasn't a fucking idiot. He knew what happened when people found out girls weren't born girls. With girl parts. Whatever.

And besides, Rob *wasn't* a girl. Wasn't born one, not physically and not even on the inside. He just liked . . . playing one. Dressing up as one.

God, was he just some twee version of dudes who wore their wives' pantyhose and lace panties for a thrill? A shy drag queen who couldn't dance?

OMG, not even, Rob. You know exactly what you are: you're an internet pervert. You're that person after-school specials in the nineties warned people about. The creepy dude who plays a sexy girl to—

What, murder them? Rape them? Get them to send money and gifts?

No way. Rob didn't want to trick anyone, and he especially didn't want to hurt anyone.

He just wanted to be a girl sometimes. Because it made him feel good. Not even sexually—okay, not *just* sexually. It just felt right. Being Bobby—part-time, at least—felt right.

And how could something that felt so right be wrong?

Which was all to say that over the last week, he'd spent more of his class time thinking about the Bobby conundrum than about his actual classwork. Oops.

Outside of class, he continued with his usual lack of a social life: he worked his shifts at Rear Entrance Video (and no, didn't see Dylan there again, although the jury was out as to whether he was relieved or disappointed about that), avoided Noah and his new girlfriend, refused invitations from his sister, did reams of homework, and lost sleep playing Kingdom of Elves.

In between all that, he worked on cobbling together a suitable girl disguise—no, outfit—to cam in. He didn't want to overdo it, so he stuck with basics: a pink Gap hoodie (oversized enough to make the question of breasts a moot point), some makeup from Sephora (for his sister, he said, which also gave him the perfect excuse to seek extra guidance from the salesgirl), a pair of cute nerdy-feminine reading glasses, and finally, a headband to try and girly up his shaggy hair.

By the time Friday had rolled around, he was so anxious he thought he was going to die. He also had the workings of what he hoped was a pretty convincing girl in his backpack.

The whole thing had cost him a couple hundred bucks, and for the first time he was pretty glad of the Rear Entrance Video job, because it meant that he was spending his own money and not his parents'. He may have talked himself out of thinking he was doing wrong by playing Bobby, but that didn't mean he was willing to spend someone else's hard-earned cash on the whole charade.

Not a charade. Not a charade. He gave himself a recriminating glare in the mirror and plucked at the chest of his pink sweatshirt, mimicking breasts a moment before rolling his eyes and letting the fabric fall. The sweatshirt was just the beginning, he reminded himself.

He was wearing his own jeans and boxers, partially because the webcam's camera was aimed above the waist, but maybe also a little bit because he was so determined to convince himself that this wasn't for kinks, never mind the fact that buying panties seemed counterproductive for someone determined not to let an innocent webcam chat with Mike turn into sex.

Nodding to himself one last time, Rob double-checked that his bedroom door was locked and got to work on the more intensive parts of his transformation.

The headband had a white satin bow, and he used it to carefully frame his hair around his face. Makeup came next: tinted moisturizer in his shade, a shimmery but very natural—the salesgirl had assured him—eye shadow, then blush.

Okay, too much blush. He scrubbed at his face with a makeup removing wipe, applied another layer of the moisturizer, and tried again. Sucked in his cheeks this time, and limited himself to one swipe of the brush.

The mascara looked a lot more daunting than it actually was, although he had to laugh at himself for gaping into the mirror bug-eyed and with his mouth hanging open in the exact same way he'd made fun of his sister for doing all these years. Once he'd gotten over his own hypocrisy, though, it was just a matter of holding the brush vaguely horizontal and then blinking on it a bunch of times.

It looked just this side of terrible on him, clumpy and spiky and not really enhancing his (admittedly sparse) lashes at all, but his webcam was shitty quality, and anyway, who said "real" girls had to be good at this? Was Bobby the kind of girl to wear false lashes? She was not, Rob decided, and put on her glasses.

The peachy-pink lip gloss was last, and it was a sticky mess . . . that also happened to look cute as hell, so he counted it as a win.

Damn! He looked fucking great, bad mascara and all. He ran his fingers through his hair, fluffing it, then raised his chin, practicing the half-swallow technique he'd read about on an MTF forum which supposedly made your Adam's apple disappear.

His technique wasn't perfect, but neither was the webcam. He could do this. He could do this. He fought down the urge to pump himself up with some jumping jacks to the *Rocky* soundtrack.

Instead, he threw himself into his computer chair and popped his headphones on over his satin headband—hmm, maybe Bobby needed some earbuds or a Bluetooth headset or something like that; something that didn't interfere with the accessorizing—and logged on to Kingdom of Elves, purring into his microphone, "Hey there, boys, ready to kill some motherfucking demon spawn?"

The raid took about three hours, and Rob practiced his Bobby voice by spending almost all three of them shouting orders and trading insults and baby-talking his way into getting more than was strictly his fair share of the loot, all in all spending far more time on voice chat than he normally ever would. Soon, though, the last rare item and gold coin had been divvied up, the last insult had been traded, the last in-joke had been recited. One by one, the members of their raid went their separate ways.

"We still on for tonight?" Mike asked into Rob's ear once they were alone.

"Of course!" Rob trilled back. "You didn't get cold feet, did you?"

"I didn't if you didn't."

"I didn't."

"So . . . Skype?"

Wow, Mike seemed just as nervous as Rob was about this whole thing. Was this where Rob found out that Mike had been a girl the whole time? Or a middle-aged man?

Would serve you right.

But then Mike's webcam invitation opened in front of him and he wasn't any of those things: he was just a very slightly pudgy white dude wearing a My Little Pony T-shirt and a huge set of expensive headphones, looking so cute and harmless it should have been criminal.

Rob swallowed his Adam's apple, took one last deep breath, and accepted the invitation.

Mike's mouth fell open, his blue eyes glued to his screen, not looking up to his webcam lens even once. Which kind of felt like he was staring at Rob's tits. A patently ridiculous assumption since he didn't have any, and what was tit-level on his end of the camera was face-level on Mike's.

"What?" Rob asked, and felt an awkward little laugh rise up in his throat.

"Wow. Just wow." Mike grinned.

"*What?*" Rob asked again, but the heat in his cheeks was all Bobby, flattered down to the tips of his toes.

"You're fucking gorgeous."

Bobby ducked his head, brushing shyly at his bangs, and wasn't it fucking weird that the fact that someone found him pretty seemed to have ten times more impact on him than the revelation that he could successfully pass? "Come on. I'm wearing a sweatshirt."

"I'm serious! You could be wearing a garbage bag and I'd still be saying that."

Bobby still couldn't look at the camera. "Yeah, well, you say that now, but you should see me in the morning," he hedged.

"Babe, I would *love* that."

O. M. G. "You did not just say what I thought you said."

"What?"

"You are totally hitting on me, Mike!"

"I'm not!"

"In what universe is 'I want to see you when you wake up in the morning' not a proposition?"

"Uh . . ."

"Yeah, caught you, didn't I? What, no comeback to that?"

"God, I'm sorry, I guess I was, wasn't I? Damn though, can you blame me? I mean, your voice is pretty cute but the real deal is even better."

Bobby laughed, drawing his knees up to his chest and hugging them. His computer chair swayed with the motion, the shut-in nerd version of a girl twisting on her ankles. "Okay, I forgive you."

"Good. So, will you forgive me if I ask you to . . ." *Now* Mike's eyes flicked up to the camera. His pupils were huge, and at this angle Bobby could see the freckles across the bridge of his nose, the twitch of his tongue flicking out to wet his lower lip. *No no no no no don't you fucking dare, don't you dare fucking finish that sentence. Don't you dare try to turn this into cheap camsex.*

Before he knew what he was even doing, Rob was X-ing out of the webcam window. Blocking Mike's accounts. Panting like he'd just dodged a fucking bullet.

"That was close," he said aloud, surprising himself with the masculine sound of his own voice.

What was close? It wasn't like Mike could force him to do anything. Rob could have just said no or changed the subject, after all. And yet saying no to Mike under false pretenses—as if Rob's refusal was for any reason other than the fact that he didn't have tits *to* show off—seemed to make his whole act feel strangely artificial, like that was just one lie too many. And then Mike's request of "Can I see your tits?" became a demand of "Prove you have them."

All those questions Rob was so afraid of people asking. All those suspicions and accusations.

Shit. Being a part-time girl was a fucking minefield.

CHAPTER 6

And yet, as precarious as it was, Rob didn't want to stop.

Because it made him feel good, dammit. Confident. Pretty. *Genuine*, somehow, as contradictory as it sounded.

He just . . . needed to find an outlet. Yeah, that.

A place where he could safely be Bobby, where there was a low likelihood of anyone recognizing that Bobby and Robert were the same person. A place where nobody knew him, at least not yet, not as Robert. A place he went regularly enough that he could get some real practice on a consistent basis. A place where, if people noticed anything off or eccentric about him, they might be more likely to shrug it off.

Which all led to Rear Entrance Video, of course.

After all, he'd only been working there a few months, and only on his own for a couple of weeks. Nobody had seen him enough to know his name or his face, he didn't think, but he was still at the store several times a week, which satisfied the consistent practice requirement. And as for the last bit, well. He was working the counter at a seedy porn store on Davie Street, at the heart of Vancouver's gay village. After last night, Rob was pretty convinced of his ability to pass, but on the off chance that he didn't, was there really anything remarkable about a cross-dressing Asian kid in that setting?

He thought not.

But if he was going to do this IRL, that meant committing to it. And committing to it meant he needed more than just a pink sweatshirt and a headband. He needed a wardrobe, one that could get him through a couple of days, one that included the stuff *below* the waist. He needed suitably girly hair. He needed . . . breasts.

So that Saturday morning, he once again begged out of his sister's post-yoga invitation. "I, uh," he said, dabbing at his sweaty throat while she stared at him with her pretty, questioning eyes. "I have to go shopping. Today."

She perked up at that, smiling and nodding. "Well, I'll go with you, then!"

Shit. Should have expected that.

"God knows you can't be trusted to dress yourself," she added, and her douchebag friend in the head-to-toe Lululemon menswear snorted.

Rob put up both hands, bowing and ducking back, desperate to escape her circle of admirers and pleading gaze. "No, no, no. You go with your friends. Have smoothies. I'm going all the way out to Metrotown, you'll end up wasting your entire day."

For every step he moved backward, though, Bernice took one forward. "It wouldn't be a waste! I could, um, go to Zara!"

"They have a Zara on Robson. No point bussing all the way out to Burnaby for that."

"Aha!" She prodded him in the chest. "But does the Zara on Robson have my kid brother there to hold my bags?"

"Uh, not selling me on your company much there, Bernie," he countered, but he realized that if he wanted to get her off his back, he was going to have to break out the big guns. Scare her off for real. "Besides. I'm already going with someone. My, uh . . . my *boyfriend.* Yeah."

Her expression glazed over, not quite comprehending, not at first, and then the realization came over her face, her mouth falling open in surprise. "Your . . . Rob! Oh my God, Rob!"

Rob wrinkled his nose, and whether it was at her overreaction or at the fact that *this* was the way he'd chosen to come out to her after all these years, he wasn't sure. "Like you didn't already know," he said. Another step back, but this time Bernice was too stunned to follow.

"Well, yeah," she stammered, "But you hadn't actually, y'know, *said* anything about it to me before this. And now you have a boyfriend?"

"Seems like a good enough reason to come out, don't you think?"

She shook her head, unimpressed, but then seemingly decided not to press the issue. "Well, what's his name? Can I meet him?"

Ah, double shit. "Uh, sometime. Maybe. Look, I gotta go, I'm running late. Don't wanna be responsible for us breaking up, do you?"

Before she could reply, Rob turned tail and ran.

On the train ride out to Metrotown in Burnaby, Rob got roughly thirty texts from Bernice, all of them begging for more details on his make-believe boyfriend, apologizing for not reacting better, wondering if he was okay, etc. He was starting to feel like an asshole, but telling any more lies, even just to support the existing ones, seemed counterproductive.

"Whoops, my battery died!" he said aloud, and turned the phone off.

Which was a bit of an asshole move on its own, now that he thought about it. Shit. Well, he'd avoid her for a couple days, lay low, and then construct a breakup as phoney as his imaginary boyfriend had ever been. As long as he didn't let the story get convoluted, it should be okay, right?

He had a sudden image of himself with an entire constructed relationship, a made-up man with made-up looks and made-up desires and made-up quirks, going on made-up dates with him, getting into made-up arguments, having made-up . . . make-ups?

Better to keep the artificial constructions in his life limited to his time on the internet. Maybe not even that, anymore. He hadn't yet figured out what to do about the whole Mike situation, but his gut was telling him to cancel his Kingdom of Elves account, or at least start afresh with a new name and a new guild. But then, maybe a couple days on blocks would cool Mike's head so he didn't push Rob's boundaries again.

And Rob wanted to be Bobby *more* of the time?

Yes, yes, he did. No matter how complicated it got, no matter what it cost, he did. He'd figure out the details.

One blessing to living in a city as liberal as Vancouver: it wasn't too much of a hardship to find a store that catered to his particular needs. The aptly named Butterflies (because they transformed into something beautiful, get it?) did a weird trade, catering to drag queens, trans girls, and cisgender women requiring weaves or wigs. Rob bypassed the shelves of flashy man-sized high heels, and went straight to the little display of silicone bra inserts. If he was going to wear anything tighter-fitting than his sweatshirt, he needed boobs for his bra. Nothing excessive, of course, but just that little something. Itty Bitty Titty Committee versus flat as a boy—er, board.

Next item: girlier hair. He stared at the wall of wigs and extensions, absolutely overwhelmed by options, until the Filipina salesgirl came to stand beside him. "Can I help you?" she asked, her sharp gaze landing on the bra inserts in his hand and then discreetly slipping away again without comment. Rob thought he'd be more embarrassed, but something about her put him at ease. He had a feeling he was hardly the first would-be cross-dresser to come across her threshold. Maybe this was the way his Rear Entrance Video customers felt.

In which case, she felt about Rob the same way Rob felt about them. Okay. He could do this. After all, getting help and guidance from a real person was the whole reason he'd come here instead of shopping online. Well, that and getting his stuff faster and without the shipping charges.

"Um, yeah, actually. I need something . . ." He circled his hand, trying to come up with the word. "For everyday, I guess? Easy to put in?"

"Something that looks natural?"

"Yeah!"

"So no pink wigs, then." She laughed, and the sound put Rob at ease.

"Not an anime character, so yeah, maybe not."

"Sure! We have nice clip-in human hair extensions. Match your color. I show you how to use them here, then you can do it yourself at home. Very easy."

She led him to one of the store's three salon chairs and he took a seat, trying not to meet the eye of the woman getting her weave sewn in in the seat next to him. Luckily, she didn't even look up from the game of Angry Birds on her phone, so Rob took a deep breath and forced himself to focus on the task at hand. He wasn't going to be ashamed. He wasn't going to be ashamed. He wasn't going to be ashamed.

The salesgirl brought him several samples, which she held up next to his face for his approval in the mirror. The language of texture and quality and human hair versus synthetic flew right over his head until finally the salesgirl clucked and asked him straight-up how much he wanted to spend. "I dunno, medium?" Rob had replied, and she'd laughed again before listing off price points.

At last they settled on a full head of shoulder-length clip-ins, black and wispy, and Rob tried not to think too hard about whatever woman had sold her hair so his dreams to be Bobby could be realized. The salesgirl walked Rob through the process of clipping them in, how to blend them into his own shaggy hair, and he sat watching as inch by inch he was transformed. He couldn't help but smile at himself. Even in his boy clothes, the long hair made him feel undeniably pretty. When he tossed it over his shoulder, the salesgirl applauded.

Rob was too busy staring at himself in a mixture of awe and vanity to notice that the salesgirl had left his side, which meant he was surprised when she reappeared again with a photocopied neon pink slip of paper.

"You take this to the hair supply store by the Bay," she told him, pressing it into his hands. It was a list of hair products to buy. Care instructions. A return policy. All of it illustrated with a grainy photo of Beyoncé that whoever ran this store almost certainly did *not* have permission to use.

He saluted her, and she was just about to lead him to the till when he caught her by the elbow. "So, uh . . . sorry for wasting your time, but can you maybe take them out now?"

She clucked at him, then smiled in apology. "Of course."

He was sad to see them go so soon, teased by his own half-fulfilled transformation, but it turned out to be a good learning opportunity, because she guided him through how to unclip them, how to keep them neat and prevent them from tangling. At last, she wrapped them in tissue paper and led him to the till. He set the bra inserts right on the counter in front of her, making no apologies and offering no explanations.

Turned out she didn't need either. "Is this all?" she asked, "You need shoes? Nails?"

The ol' upsell, same as Rob asking if people wanted batteries or lube with that.

It was easy, after that, to buy his girl clothes at the Chinese mall across the street from Metrotown. Easy even to buy bras, especially since he'd read a how-to on the internet and figured out his nonexistent cup size the night before. 34AA. He'd thought he'd have to offer up some excuse about buying them for a women's center, or for his kid sister, or his girlfriend, anything but letting the salesgirl think he was some kind of sex pervert, but the confidence of those few minutes of seeing himself in the mirror with Bobby's beautiful hair carried him through.

When he'd reached the end of his list, he had an early dinner at the mall food court (mmm, food court pho), and hopped on the train back downtown, not just ready but excited for his first Bobby-shift at Rear Entrance Video.

No apologies. No explanations.

CHAPTER 7

"**Y**ou're gonna be okay here on your own?" Noah asked, still lingering halfway out the door like he was afraid to leave. The guy had some serious puppy dog face going on, like he'd been hit on the nose with the newspaper one too many times.

"Um, of course?" Rob, sitting behind the counter, forced himself to smile. Wow, things between them had gotten awkward lately, and for what, because Rob was jealous of Noah's new girlfriend? Well, *Bobby* sure as hell wouldn't get all weird—plenty of fish in the metaphorical sea, and if Noah didn't realize how amazing Bobby was, then the dude didn't deserve him in the first place—so Rob wasn't going to be that way either.

There. Resolved. His next smile was more genuine. "Seriously, go. It's your night off, isn't it? You going out with Jenny?"

Noah must have keyed into the lack of bitterness in Rob's voice, or maybe the thought of Jenny just made him that happy, because he *beamed.* "Yeah. Yeah, I am."

Rob flapped his hands at him. "Then go! Go-go-go!"

But just as he was about to leave, Noah paused. Half turned. "So we're cool? You and me?"

Thanks to that bit of Bobby inside him, they really, really were. "Yeah." Rob smiled. "We are."

"Good. Goodgoodgood. Okay. Going." Damn, Noah had it *bad.* Rob gave him a jaunty wave, almost enjoying Noah's dopey puppy love all of a sudden, and then he was gone.

Right. Time to set his plan into action. He put up the *Back in 15 Minutes* sign, grabbed his bag out from under the front counter, and hurried to the bathroom at the back of the store. Locked the door behind him.

Stripped naked in more ways than one, he stared down at his backpack. Funny, how everything he needed to bring Bobby into existence—a massive, maybe even life-altering transformation—all fit into one measly bag.

Well, one measly bag, plus Rob's own spirit. After all, without the breath of Bobby inside him, all he had here was a bag of clothes and hair.

Jeez, he was getting kinda philosophical about all this, wasn't he? And he only had fifteen minutes, at least according to the sign. God only knew if Charlie VIP was standing outside the door right now, anxious to be let in. Or Sweatpants-and-boner Guy, pounding down the door with his dick.

Bra and panties first. Rob tore the tags off them, fumbled with the bra a bit before figuring out the trick of doing up the hooks and eyes in the front of his chest first and *then* spinning the bra around and slipping his arms through the straps, and then stepped into the matching panties. Couldn't help cupping his soft dick and balls through the floral pink cotton with its lace edging. No denying it, he loved the look of it, the way he filled out the front of the panties, nearly overflowing them, a bulge they weren't meant to take but that looked so fucking good.

As sexually attractive as it made him feel, though, it wouldn't do much for the "passing" part of his act once he put on the tight girls' jeans. Luckily, a helpful explanation on how to tuck without the use of tape was a quick phone search away—thanks, Jennifer Ann!—and once the panties were on again, their tight fabric held everything in place. He made a mental note to buy some medical tape next time he was anywhere near a drugstore.

He stroked his newly smooth front absentmindedly for a minute or two, then remembered his fifteen minute limit, now down to nearly ten. The chicken fillet silicone bra inserts came next, and then there was a bit more adjusting in the mirror, trying to get them to sit right inside his bra. After that, the clothes were easy—jeans and shirts were jeans and shirts, boy or girl—and the makeup was easier the second time around as well. Last of all, he clipped in his extensions, cursing the whole time because of course getting the fucking things attached to his hair and lying right and looking okay was about a thousand times harder than the salesgirl had made it look, and fuck, he was already into minute twenty of his fifteen minutes, *God fucking dammit*.

But suddenly the last section of hair clipped and everything *clicked*, and Rob was staring at himself in the mirror and seeing Bobby staring back.

And God, she was fucking beautiful.

Of course he started crying after that; pretty girl tears that had mascara streaking down across his perfectly foundation-ed and blush-ed cheeks. Maybe he should have been frustrated by that, ruining his makeup all for a stupid happy-cry, but crying like a girl, right down to the messed makeup, just made him even happier. Because suddenly it was all *real*. Real, and so much better than he ever could have hoped.

Smiling anew, Bobby rooted through his makeup bag for something to fix his runny mascara.

CHAPTER 8

Funnily enough, Charlie VIP actually *was* outside when Bobby finally put on his glasses and made it to the front door twenty-five minutes after hanging the *Back in 15 Minutes* sign.

"Oh, hello, miss," Charlie said, stepping in while Bobby held the door open. "Back door was locked, so I came around to the front and *it* was locked, too. Thought you were never gonna open up."

Bobby half-swallowed his Adam's apple and spoke. "Sorry, sir. I was just . . ." *No point lying.* "Fixing my makeup. How do I look?" He batted his sticky eyelashes. God*damn* he sucked at mascara. Maybe tonight he'd look up some tutorials on YouTube.

"Pretty as a geisha," Charlie replied, pronouncing it gee-shah.

Uh, yikes. Mental note: don't ask creepers for compliments, because their compliments are just as creepy as the rest of them. "Thanks!" he chirped, fleeing for the counter. "Let me know if you need any help."

It was more of a formality than anything: Charlie VIP knew what he liked and where to find it. Five or ten minutes from now, he'd come ambling up to the counter with his German fisting fetish DVDs, Bobby would ring him through, and then he'd be on his merry way.

Which was why it surprised Bobby when Charlie followed him to the counter almost immediately. "Yes?" Bobby asked, smiling as sweetly as he could. He hoped he hadn't opened a door he couldn't close with the whole fishing-for-a-compliment thing.

Charlie gave him a shifty-eyed look. "You said to let you know if I need any help. Well, I need help."

"Oh! Um! Okay, sure, what can I help you with?" More nicey-nice smiles.

"Can you suggest a DVD for me?"

"Of course, sir." Bobby summoned up his knowledge of popular rentals in the various sections of the store. "What were you thinking of?"

"I'd like you to tell me the most erotic film you've ever seen."

What? "Excuse me?"

"I'd like you to tell me the most erotic film you've ever seen."

Jesus. Creeper taking creepy to a whole new level. Just get rid of him. Pick whatever. "Sure!" Bobby stood, flipping a lock of hair over his shoulder. He led Charlie into the Anal section, scanning the shelves until he found the title he wanted, a double-penetration video that had crossed the counter on more than one shift. "How about this?"

"Do you like that?" Charlie asked.

"A lot of people like it. It goes out all the time. I think this actress is really popular."

Charlie didn't seem impressed with that answer. "I asked, did *you* like it."

Jeez. Awkward. Bobby couldn't exactly say he didn't watch porn, but he wasn't sure if his current passing status would hold up if he admitted to liking gay porn. Also, he didn't really *want* to tell Charlie VIP what got him off, period. *Just get rid of him.* "Oh, yes, sir."

"What, exactly, did you like about it?"

Oh God ew, is he trying to dirty-talk with me? Charlie hadn't touched him, but Bobby's skin still crawled. "It has a pretty great soundtrack." Which was true, strangely enough. Bobby had been doing some reading up in order to be less useless in the area of customer service, and this director was well known for directing his porn like music videos.

Not surprisingly, Charlie's whole face curled up in disgust.

"And it has double penetration," Bobby added.

"Eh, that's pretty tame for me." Of course it was. Honestly, at this point Bobby doubted anything short of scat or bestiality could really hope to make its way through Charlie's porn-desensitized shields. And for now, he seemed completely disheartened as he put the DP video back on the shelf and wandered off to the Fetish section alone, leaving Bobby to skulk back to the counter.

It was an awkward resolution to the whole situation, but at least things went partway back to normal after that. Charlie rented three of his usual DVDs, bid Bobby goodnight, and left. The next customer came in on his heels, a woman looking for a remote control vibrator for her and her girlfriend, and Bobby had a great time showing her the different options and joking about the sleazy packaging and the inherent lack of eroticism involved in strapping an insect to one's genitals. At last, she chose one that didn't come with any kind of straps or harnesses, but looked as if it could be held in place with a combination of insertion and wearing it with tight panties so it wouldn't slip out. By the time she left, Bobby was grinning ear to ear, buoyed by the pure and simple joy of girl talk. Honest-to-God girl talk. Maybe his sister was right about the female friends thing. Too bad Bobby couldn't accept her frequent invites on Rob's behalf.

Except for the thing with Charlie, the night passed in a pleasant pattern of harmless flirtation, a lot of which Bobby initiated himself to ease his customers' nerves. He couldn't really blame the guys: it must be weird to have to show your taste in porn to a woman you didn't even know. Luckily, an easy smile and a cute line seemed to work wonders, even on Hollister Cap Guy, who showed up solo midshift and politely signed up for a membership card. Bobby could have done without the meaningful waggle of the eyebrows as the guy slid a stack of Asian fetish DVDs across the counter at him, but the encounter was roughly five thousand times less unpleasant than their last one.

And Bobby couldn't help feeling a sense of victory when Hollister Cap Guy—real name Adam Fickes—left the store not with an extended middle finger, but a scribbled phone number on his receipt and a sweet, eager "Call me!" Bobby balled up the receipt and tossed it in the trash, of course, but it still felt fucking good.

When things at the store slowed down, Bobby got caught up on his homework, although he spent half of that time fantasizing about how different his classes could be if Bobby were taking them instead of stupid, social-reject Rob. Maybe Bobby could join the cardigan club, or learn to knit, or maybe he could sit at the back of the class with Dylan, flirting and goofing off. After all, Rob had to try hard, had to work hard, had to just keep his head down. Bobby didn't have to do any of those things. Bobby had fun. Made friends. Seduced boys. Was totally kickass and capable at the same time, but in a completely sexy, effortless way.

The bell over the door chimed, and Bobby, still floating on the cotton candy cloud of his fantasies, looked up with a smile.

"Holy shit!" Dylan ERASE RACISM shouted.

Bobby squeaked, a deer in fucking headlights with nowhere to go and nowhere to hide. Nothing to say. Well, he could shout "I can explain!" but then he'd have to actually follow it up with an explanation, and he sure as hell didn't have one of those to spare.

"They actually employ girls here?"

What? "What?"

There it was, that squeak again.

"Oh, shit, sorry. There goes my mouth again." Dylan laughed. "I didn't mean to make you feel all awkward, it's just that every time I've come in here, it's been a dude behind the counter. Total sausage fest."

Was this seriously happening right now? Was Dylan seriously not recognizing him for the ridiculous little cross-dresser he was? Was Dylan seriously buying that he was a real girl and, y'know, *not his fucking classmate that he'd seen at least ten times*? Maybe it was the glasses. Yeah. Had to be the glasses. And the hair. The hair probably helped.

"Um, yeah. Hi. I'm Bobby." *Real smooth.* "And yes, I'm a girl." *Real smoother.* "No sausages here." *Real smoothest, and oh, also? A lie.*

Dylan chuckled to himself, but it wasn't a judgmental laugh. "Well, hello to you, Bobby. I'm Dylan."

Bobby's face flushed right up to the hairline, like he'd just drunk three bottles of beer. "Hi."

Dylan cocked an eyebrow, repeating back, "Hi."

Wow, turned at this three-quarters angle, his round face transformed into a more complicated shape, smooth but for his high, sharp cheekbones. "Hi," Bobby breathed.

"Hi," Dylan said again, and grinned.

"Oh. Jesus, I'm sorry, this is like a bad romantic comedy." Bobby shook his head, tossing his hair. Cleared his throat. "God. Okay, well, I'm going to stop talking now before I embarrass myself. More. Than I have already."

Dylan laughed, a dry, deep sound that was worldly and kind, nothing like the cruel laugh he sometimes used at school when one of their classmates said something particularly stupid. Damn, it sounded good. "Sure, okay," he said.

Bobby pinched his knees together, heat creeping through his skin down there, too. "Let me know if you need anything? Or you can just let me crawl under this counter and die."

"If you die, is my porn free?"

Now it was Bobby's turn to laugh, a sound that was suitably feminine but nothing like the practiced giggles he'd used on Mike.

"Is that a yes?"

"Oh my God, just go away already, would you?" Bobby covered his red-hot face with his hands, even shaking his head back and forth a little. "Preferably somewhere that there's a high shelf blocking the view between us."

"Sure thing, ma'am," Dylan said with a wry grin, and pointedly walked behind the nearest tall shelf, the rack of blowjob videos, and out of sight. And after a few *looooong* minutes, called out, "Bobby, can I come out now? There's no gay stuff behind here."

Bobby snorted. "Fine, fine."

"Sorry, does me being gay ruin your romantic comedy?" Dylan asked as he reappeared from behind the blowjob shelf and made his way to the gay section.

Not as much as you think. "Yeah, but I think I'll survive." Bobby rolled his eyes, putting his chin in his hand.

"Ouch. Damn, girl, that was cold."

"You started it."

"Hey, who's Christian?" From his place over at the shelf, Dylan held up a DVD case for Bobby to see, one of the ones with Christian's cheesy *Staff Pick* sticker on it. Bobby most certainly hadn't participated in that little exercise.

"The manager here."

"He's into tattoos, huh? Piercings? Twinks?"

"Check, check, and check. And his boyfriend's got all three."

"His boyfriend's got twinks?"

Bobby flapped his hand dismissively. "You know what I mean. *Got* tattoos and piercings. *Is* a twink."

"Uh-huh. And what about you, Miss Bobby? What are you into?" Funny, but even though Charlie VIP had basically asked the same question, it felt completely different coming from Dylan.

And maybe because of that, Bobby didn't mind replying honestly. "I'm a bit of a chubby chaser, actually."

"Oh? So you like all this?" Dylan lifted his baggy sweatshirt and grabbed two fistfuls of his bare—but not all that chubby—belly.

"I thought you were gay?" Which wasn't to say that Bobby didn't like what Dylan was packing, because yeah, he did. All round and smooth and such a sexy deep brown . . . Not to mention that sparse hint of hair peeking over the tops of his boxers. Mmm, man-hair. Dylan might not have much, but he had it where it counted.

Dylan pulled his shirt back down, ruining Bobby's view. "What, just 'cause I'm gay, I can't fish for compliments from a cute girl?"

"You think I'm cute?" Bobby clapped a hand over his mouth. Nope, definitely hadn't meant to say that aloud. Especially not in an earnest, flattered squeak.

"Definitely," Dylan said, and sauntered up to the counter with his selection. "And you work at a porn store, which makes you cool. Cool and cute. Deadly combo, even for a homo like me."

There was that blush again. Bobby snatched Dylan's DVD case—a Mischievous Pictures title, nice, and Vancouver-based to boot—off the counter and spun to the filing cabinets full of discs, hoping he'd done it fast enough that Dylan hadn't noticed his expression.

"Aren't you gonna compliment me back?" he said when Bobby turned around again. He was leaning on his elbows on the counter, smiling a wicked smile, eyelids low. Oh yeah, he'd seen Bobby's expression all right. At least he wasn't rubbing Bobby's face in it.

"Sure!" Bobby replied, feeling a hundred times less shy and awkward now that he knew Dylan wasn't going to give him a hard time. He smiled, baring teeth, as he put down Dylan's rental disc. "You have great taste in gay porn."

"Tell me something I don't know," Dylan snorted, and handed over his member card and cash.

I'm secretly a dude. "Velociraptors had feathers," Bobby said. "This is due back—"

"Thursday. Yeah. See you around, Bobby."

And oh, the sound of his name in that voice, barely clipped by an accent. "Yeah," Bobby said, all dreamy. "See ya Monday, Dylan."

Dylan raised both eyebrows at him. "Thursday, Bobby. It's due back *Thursday.*"

Ah, shit. Not crossing the streams was about to get ten thousand times harder.

On Monday morning, those lines blurred further when Rob walked into class, looked right into Dylan's eyes, and smiled.

Because whoa now, Robert Ng never made eye contact with *anybody* first, and he especially didn't act all familiar. After all, it had been Dylan and *Bobby* who'd flirted back and forth at Rear Entrance Video on Saturday night. Dylan and Robert, on the other hand, had barely traded two words, and none of them in the classroom setting.

Luckily, Dylan just smiled back, even tossed Rob a wave, like it was a totally normal thing for strangers to smile and wave at each other and not weird in the slightest.

Phew.

And then, once Doctor Chastity had arrived and started the day's lecture, there were more exchanged glances: smiles and shrugs and head tilts and eyebrow raisings and pursings of lips. Every time Rob looked in Dylan's direction, there was Dylan looking right back at him. Watching him? Watching him closely? Too closely? Did he suspect?

No, you fucking idiot. It's because you greeted him when you came in, and he doesn't have anyone else in this class to talk to, just like you.

After all, if he hadn't made the connection between Rob and Bobby in all that time they'd talked the other night, then he never would. Right?

And if he knew, would he really be smiling at Rob right now?

No way. Frowning, curious, grossed out, maybe.

But definitely not smiling.

OMG, stop looking at him.

Rob turned away quickly, tucking his chin into his hand and his eyes behind his bangs. On the desk in front of him, his notes were embarrassingly bad: half-finished words, sentences that went nowhere, weird little boxes and stars he didn't remember drawing. His head felt like it was about to float right off of his shoulders. God, he hoped whatever Doctor Chastity was teaching today wasn't important.

Oh, who was he kidding, it was *Introduction to Art Principles.* How important could it be?

"—So you'll be needing a partner."

That important, apparently. Yikes.

Bewildered and helpless, Rob took a look over both shoulders, watching the class's various cliques divide into smaller subgroups, like cells splitting. There was no awkwardness, no deliberation, nothing. Everybody was already sitting near their partners, so there was even a minimum of chair scraping. One second, he'd been lost in his Dylan-related fantasy-slash-anxiety-spiral, and the next, everyone in his class was paired off in their little huddles, chatting excitedly.

Everyone but Rob.

And Dylan.

Who wasn't getting up, wasn't making any move to approach Rob, wasn't even smiling like he'd been doing all through class. Now he was sitting back in his chair, feet up on his desk, pointedly *not* looking at Rob.

Well, maybe the pairs requirement was more of a guideline. Maybe Rob could just ask to work alone, make up some excuse about social anxiety that hopefully someone like Doctor Chastity would accept as genuine and valid.

Or Rob could take a page from Bobby's book and just fucking walk up to the guy, sit down next to him, not even ask for permission to be partners, just fucking *own* it.

Just pretend to be Bobby. Without the hair, or the glasses, or the voice, or anything that made Bobby the cute go-getter she was.

This was a disaster. This was a fucking disaster waiting to happen. No, it was a disaster *already happening* and, oh God, when had Rob gotten to his feet and started walking over to Dylan? He hadn't decided to walk over to Dylan, had he? How was he already halfway across the classroom when he hadn't even decided to go there? Could he still turn around? Pretend he'd meant to go to the bathroom? God, no, that would look so lame and there was no way he could get away with it. No way—

"Hey," Dylan said, pulling out the chair next to his own.

Oh. Well. That wasn't so bad.

"Hey," Rob replied. Okay, nothing too weird there, either. Good start. Keep it going. "So, I, uh . . . I didn't actually hear why we were pairing up?"

"And here I thought you were a front row keener," Dylan said, a twinkle in his eyes.

And even though it was clearly meant as harmless teasing, Rob couldn't help but bristle. *You don't know me at all.*

"Aaanyway. We're supposed to do this gallery tour . . . thing. I'm Dylan, by the way."

"Yeah, I know," Rob said, and immediately started to blush.

"Didn't know I made that much of an impression."

Yeah, well, apparently I haven't made much of one on you.

"I'm Rob, by the way."

"Yeah, I know," Dylan mimicked, bobbing his head side to side with a sneer.

"You do not. You're just trying—"

"Rob Ng. N-G, pronounced like I-N-G." Dylan gave him a smug stare. "Ceramics, right?"

"Oh. Uh. Yeah."

"Dude, don't get all weirded out, it's not like I have a shrine to you in my closet or something. Just a good memory for faces, that's all."

Hmm, well, it was true that Dylan had surprised him once, but Rob had an inkling his memory for faces wasn't *quite* as good as he thought if he could be tricked by a pair of glasses and some hair extensions.

Unless, of course, he hadn't been tricked.

Rob stared at him hard, trying to find any hint in his expression—a smile, maybe, a crinkle at the corner of his eyes, a sneer?—that Dylan knew about Bobby. But there was nothing, just Dylan's big round face, completely open and completely Bobby-awareness-free.

Which made sense, of course. Hadn't Rob pinned Dylan as someone with no filter, right on that first night they'd met, when Dylan had gone off on some tangent about his sister's porn career? Was the guy even capable of keeping a secret?

Rob thought not.

"So, gallery tour?" he said.

"Were you just checked out of this entire class? Are you some kind of secret super slacker?" Dylan teased, but he was grinning like a maniac, so Rob didn't bother apologizing.

"Kinda, yeah. In my defense, I do feel like I have a cold coming on, but, uh . . . in the interests of transparency, I also have a Kingdom of Elves account."

Dylan punched his palm, the motion like a valve for his excess energy. "No shit, man, me too! Well, I did. They lost me on that last expansion . . . racist fucking panda army. Well, that, and the subscription fees were killing me."

Rob tapped his cheek with his index finger, turning his eyes ceiling-ward. "Aw, the pandas aren't all that bad. They just speak English worse than Jackie Chan . . . and are all martial artists . . ."

Dylan raised an eyebrow, and used his palms to mimic scales weighing invisible racism.

"Well, at least they don't have cars to crash into shit," Rob finished with a grin.

"My man, you set a low bar," Dylan said, almost like it was a compliment, and clapped Rob on the shoulder companionably. "Anyway, I'd really like to get a head start on this assignment, so are you free to maybe go to the gallery tonight? The one in Surrey has a pop art exhibit. You're not busy, are you? No raids or anything?"

Not since Mike, not that Rob was going to admit that aloud. "Nah, I'm taking a break right now, focusing on school and work."

Dylan bobbed his head, like he was only half listening, and the other half was music with a rapid beat. "Cool, cool, okay, so tonight? Or hey, we could just meet up after class, get some dinner, then hop a bus?"

Dinner? Art? With *Dylan*? Rob found himself nodding back before he'd even considered the implications.

"Great, so it's a date, then," Dylan said.

It's a date.

It's a date?

Shit.

CHAPTER 9

By the end of the day's classes, Rob had obsessed enough over Dylan's phrasing that "date" didn't even sound like a word anymore. It had split into two syllables, stretched out, had a long a and a short a, had morphed into four individual letters that didn't come together at all, swimming around in his head like all the Chinese characters he'd never bothered to learn . . . And after all that, he still wasn't any closer to understanding what Dylan wanted from him.

Never mind Dylan, did Rob even know what *he* wanted? Did he want it to be a date? Sure, there was the evidence that he'd been relieved that Max was working the night shift tonight, leaving him free to accept the invitation. Rob was lonely, after all, especially without his guild-mates on Kingdom of Elves, but did he want to do the whole dating thing with Dylan, specifically? And the timing? Thanks to his adventures in cross-dressing, Rob's life was a confusing fucking mess. Even so, Dylan was one constant *in* that mess, the sole person who'd seen Rob in both roles. And not only that, whether he was with Bobby or Rob didn't change Dylan at all. He was just as flirtatious, just as funny, just as completely uncensored.

Rob . . . liked that. There was no guarantee that Dylan would continue that behavior if he ever found out that Rob and Bobby were one and the same, mind you, but in the meantime it felt so much more *genuine* than anyone else. Even a socially challenged creep like Charlie VIP had changed his behaviour when faced with one or the other, not to mention Hollister Cap Guy's complete 180 from abusive toolbag to friendly but fetishizing one.

Dylan was different. Rob or Bobby, he was the same dead honest, refreshingly plain-faced guy, with the same jokes and inexplicable flirtation and inability to control his mind-to-mouth processes.

No pretence. No act. No hidden bias, positive *or* negative.

Ah, shit. Rob was *into* him. Not to the point of doodling their names on his Trapper Keeper, but the prognosis on that front wasn't good.

Rob was doomed, in other words.

But when he looked up from slotting away the afternoon's work in student storage and saw Dylan standing in the door of the studio, hands in his pockets and head tilted, waiting for him to finish up, Rob couldn't help but think that maybe doomed was too harsh a word for it.

Destined, maybe?

Damn, cheesy.

He flashed Dylan a tight smile, hoping it didn't give anything away or suggest anything Dylan didn't want it to suggest, and finished packing his bag. Took a deep breath. Whether this was a Date or not, he'd let Dylan make the first move. Thankfully, he knew just the way to test the date factor. Slinging his bag over his shoulder, he walked straight up to Dylan like a man not ashamed or nervous of anything, and before Dylan could get a word in edgewise, he said, "So! Dinner. Ninety-nine cent pizza?"

Totally not date food. If Dylan refused it, well then—

"Fuck yeah, sounds great. I know a place that does huge slices. Big as *your* puny head."

Not a date then. Of course not. Shit, why had he ever even thought that? This was a class assignment, for fuck's sake. Going out to dinner first just made sense when the alternative was to go home and eat and then try to arrange to meet up later. Going straight from school to food to gallery was just a measure to prevent group-mates from flaking. Of course.

Inwardly, Rob fought back from collapsing like an imploding star into the black pit of disappointment sitting where his stomach should be, but outwardly, without even thinking, he riffed back, "Puny? You think this is puny? This is normal—although maybe not to a bobblehead like you." He rapidly tilted his head back and forth on his neck to illustrate, and it was only when Dylan started laughing that he realized. He'd joked back. Joined in. Been a normal, social human being. And it hadn't been painful at all.

Was that Bobby's influence on him, he wondered?
Or Dylan's?

Turned out, the pizza slices *were* the size of Rob's—totally not puny at all, thanks—head. And delicious, too, even tasted through a stuffed nose. Dylan got his slice fully loaded and slathered in that garlic sauce in the squeeze bottle. Rob, a little less adventurous, had pepperoni and cheese, picking off the pepperoni and eating it first as Dylan talked his ear off.

"Me, I grew up in a small town, almost all white—except for me and my sister of course," Dylan said through a mouthful of green peppers and potent garlic, in response to Rob's boring-ass Vancouver born n' raised spiel. "I felt like . . . well, half the time I felt like an ambassador, and the other half I felt like a prisoner of war, you know? People watching me like I'm some oddity, wishing they could just take notes while I sat in a cage. And I mean, I got good parents, and I did good in school and didn't get into any kind of trouble, so at some point people stopped expecting me to break their windows and started expecting me to be some Iron Eyes Cody model Indian for them instead, and I still don't know which was worse."

He paused, took a bite of his pizza, chewed once, and continued, the perceptiveness of his words completely at odds with the fact that Rob could see the half-masticated pizza crust rolling around over his tongue. "I don't think having white parents fucked me up, exactly, but it made me kind of mad because, you know, white government and white people put me where I was—I'm one of the last 'sixties scoop' kids. Which, you know, obviously I was adopted out in the eighties when I was a toddler, but I guess 'sixties, seventies, and eighties scoop' isn't as catchy."

Rob must have given him a blank look, because he took a moment to chew and gather his words, then explained, "Back before the current laws about Aboriginal adoptions, the government pawned off all the little Indian kids on nice white families because they couldn't do the whole government-sanctioned-child-rape thing they call 'residential schools' anymore."

"Oh." Rob had invited the explanation, but it was still a hard thing to take that in. He'd heard about residential schools in history class, of course, but he'd never heard them described that way, so bluntly—or taken so personally. But then, what did some middle-aged white dude like his high school history teacher know about what it felt like to grow up Native, carrying that inherited hurt around in your heart? No more than he knew about how it felt for Rob to listen to his classmates coolly justifying racist immigration policies targeted at "job-stealing coolies" like him and his father.

"So, anyway," Dylan continued, shrugging off that particular pain in a shockingly practiced way, "after purposely kidnapping me away from my bio-family and my home and my culture, these same white people magically expected me to turn into some kinda perfect model of . . ." He didn't finish his sentence, just made a frustrated animal noise and took a big gulp of his pop.

"Hmm," Rob said, because *That sucks* seemed pretty minimizing and *I get you* had to be a lie. But Dylan was sitting there staring at him expectantly, waiting for a reply. "Well, uh, I mean, no shortage of Chinese culture in Vancouver to pick up on, or even Chinese-Canadian, but I guess you could say even though my dad moved here back in the seventies of his own free will, it's still mine and my sister's fault if we act too Canadian."

Dylan nodded thoughtfully, and even though he wasn't speaking, he was still chewing with his mouth open. "I guess because I'm not a total screw-up, people want me to be their Good Inuit or whatever, but it turns out that other than the skin and the card and the bio-family across the country, I'm as white as they are. Except when I'm not white enough, you know? And don't get me wrong, I'm not *ashamed* of who I am or where I come or anything, I just—if I decide to embrace that and get into the Indigenous art scene or pull a Dave Chappelle and take a sabbatical in Nunavut, I want to do it because that comes from inside *me*, not because some white people think I should."

Which explained the hostility toward the soapstone carving, Rob supposed. He wondered how many times Dylan had been asked that, *Oh, you're going to art school? Are you doing your traditional art, then?*

It'd be like assuming Rob was just there to do inkbrush paintings or whatever. "Yeah," he said with a nod.

"That's why I like you, Rob; you don't do what's expected of *you*, either. White people look at you, and you say you're in school and working part-time and they probably think you're studying business or math or pre-med while you work at your parents' restaurant or something, and there you are doing ceramics and working at a porn store."

Just then, a piece of pepperoni must have decided to get all balled up in Rob's throat, because he coughed loud and hard, tears pricking up in the corners of his eyes. He took a chug of his watered-down fountain pop and spluttered and wiped his eyes and croaked out, "Wh-what?"

"Are you . . . are you okay?" Dylan asked, and Rob waved off his concerned hand reaching out to pat him on the shoulder. At his silent, watery-eyed nod, Dylan went on. "Don't you remember? I came in a few weeks back and got all weird trying to justify why I was going to a store and not getting it on the internet like a normal dude."

OhthankGod. "Oh yeah, that's right. Your sister works in the industry, right?"

"Yeah," Dylan said, settling back in his seat again and seeming pleased that Rob had remembered him after all. "Sorry if I freaked you out that night. And sorry for pretending I didn't know you when we were in class. I just wasn't sure if knowing I knew would weird you out even more."

So you kept your distance and waited for me to make the first move. "Aww, that's sweet! You're looking out for me."

"Dylan Ford knows how to be discreet!" Dylan announced with pride, tapping his nose.

Rob snorted. "Uh-huh? So what's your sister's stage name, again?"

"Ha-ha." Dylan folded his arms over his chest. "S'not indiscretion if the person doesn't mind who knows it."

"Point," Rob said. Dylan hadn't said as much, maybe was too nice to point it out, but it was really shitty of Rob to assume she'd be keeping her career a big dark secret. She didn't have to keep it a secret if she didn't want; she had nothing to be ashamed of.

"You really wanna know, though? What you gonna do, look her up in your little computer system, watch her videos and picture me instead?"

Rob resisted the urge to spit out his mouthful of pizza in disgust. "That is fucking vile, Dylan."

Dylan smiled sheepishly. "It kinda was, wasn't it? Damn, here I was just trying to flirt and instead I get all *Flowers in the Attic* on your ass."

Flirt. It was all Rob could do to keep from outright melting. "And—like the fact that both of us have apparently read that crazy chick book—let us never speak of it again."

"Deal," Dylan said, and they both reached over the table and shook on it.

CHAPTER 10

I t was twilight by the time they reached the gallery almost two hours later, and there was a light but ice-cold drizzle in the air. Dylan stepped off the bus and pulled his hood over his ears, his body vibrating with something that seemed halfway between a shiver and a wet dog shaking off. Rob, behind him, dug through his bag and pulled out his compact umbrella. Took his steps two at a time until he could open it over both their heads.

Dylan turned, his look of genuine surprise quickly shifting into a wry smile as he pulled his hood from his head. "What a gentleman!"

"Just you wait," Rob said with a wink. "Because once we get inside, I'm buying you a coffee, too."

"What? What the hell for?" Dylan's face turned tense, and he picked up his pace as they crossed the parking lot together, as if trying to escape the shelter of Rob's umbrella.

"As a thank-you for the stimulating conversation? For getting me out of my shell? To bribe you into being my friend?" Ah, that last one was supposed to sound self-deprecating, but it had come out pathetic and desperate instead. Rob fell back a step, letting Dylan make his intended escape, but instead of taking off, Dylan just stopped and turned and squinted at Rob through the rain dripping from his hair.

"You don't have to bribe me, Rob. I mean, for someone doing ceramics, you're actually pretty cool."

"Oh, um." Rob blinked. Shook his head. Dashed forward and held his umbrella up high so it covered Dylan again. "Thanks. I think you're cool too."

"Shit, I don't need *you* to tell me I'm cool. I am so cool. For one, I draw indie comics. For two, have you seen these sneakers?" He held a leg out for Rob to see. His sneakers were huge skate shoes, the kind that'd been popular in the early 2000s, two sizes too big and worn absolutely ragged, with wagging fat tongues and undone laces. They looked like absolute shit. "Had these since high school," he said proudly.

"I have no idea how those make you cool, but you have a point on the comics thing, so I guess I'll have to take your word for it."

"Yeah, guess you will." Dylan put his foot down and started walking. "And about this coffee thing . . . you know I'm gay, right?"

"Uh . . . Yeah? I kinda guessed from seeing your jerkoff material. And since you can't see what I jerk off to, I'll level the playing field. I'm gay too. But what does that have to do with the coffee?"

Dylan got to the front door of the gallery first, and stood aside, holding it open for Rob to walk through. "Just putting it out there."

Well, that didn't clarify things *at all*. Rob frowned, pretending to be superfocused on the task of shaking out and folding up his umbrella. Was Dylan warning Rob that buying him coffee would turn this into a date? Was that the signal Rob was sending, in Dylan's eyes? Did Dylan mind that Rob was sending date signals? What in God's name was Dylan "putting out there"?

Shit, Rob had no idea what was going on or what the guy meant. How could a man who spoke every single thing that crossed his mind somehow be so damn impossible to read? Of course, Rob could just ask him straight up; after all, Dylan would almost certainly answer honestly if faced with a direct question. Not that Rob could get up the guts to ask it.

So instead, he tried, "So why Pop Art? There are so many galleries downtown, even the VAG. Why bus all the way out to Surrey?"

They walked right past the shuttered coffee shop—and everything it represented—and into the main atrium of the gallery, where a permanent collection of ceramic and sculptural pieces were on display inside little glass boxes. Sterile. Untouchable.

Dylan walked by them all like he didn't even see them. "Because when we do our presentation next week they're going to be expecting me to walk up there and talk about Coast Salish art or something. Blah, blah, blah traditions, blah, blah, blah authenticity and all that shit—never mind the fact that whether you count me as Inuit or white or something in between, they're still not *my* traditions—but instead

I'm gonna go up there and tell them about neon, mass-produced American art depicting decades-old pop culture, and present it as being just as authentic as *The Raven and the First Men* ever was."

Rob stopped just before the entryway into the Visiting Collections wing where the Pop Art exhibit was housed. "You know Bill Reid?"

Dylan rolled his eyes. "Dude. I'm all bitter and possibly-almost-certainly having an existential crisis. I'm not *ignorant*."

"Sorry," Rob said.

"Apology accepted," Dylan replied, and led the way into the gallery.

If the conversation hadn't ended then, it would have when Rob finally passed the threshold and found himself face-to-face with a massive wall of brightly colored Marilyns, the image and the impact so much *more* than any college dorm poster representation could hope to be. It knocked the breath out of him. "Wow," he said, staring at all that color and contrast, his eyes unable to keep still on one single horizon. "It's big."

Dylan laughed, the sound reverberating against the gallery's white walls and high ceilings. "Yeah. And in your fucking face, right? Love it or hate it, you sure as fuck can't ignore it." He crossed his arms, his face in profile absolutely *glowing* with admiration, and then said, softer, "That's what I want for my art."

Rob wet his lips with his tongue, looking back to the images again, even though they'd lost some of their lustre in the face of the passion glinting in Dylan's black eyes. "You . . . you're not afraid of being hated?" he asked, mirroring Dylan's awed softness.

"Who are you kidding, I'm already hated. Better to be hated for something I create than for my genetics. My heritage. Whatever." The fierceness flared up hot but faded just as fast in a boom like a backdraft. "Anyway, don't you want to make an impression? Be memorable?"

"No," Rob said, rubbing his hands. At least this soon after being outside there was a possibility of the gesture being because of the cold instead of anxiety. "Useful. Well-loved. Old and cherished even if nobody quite knows why." Now it was Rob's turn to catch Dylan staring at *him*, something unreadable but undeniably attracted in his eyes. "Anyway, um, we should . . . we should probably start taking some notes for this tour."

"Y-yeah," Dylan said. And what was that unsteady waver in his voice?

After the coffee fiasco, Rob refused to analyze it. Instead, he followed Dylan's meandering path through the gallery, letting Dylan take the lead on describing and analyzing the pieces while he hung back and wrote notes. He'd put it all together in a PowerPoint presentation tonight, and then he'd shunt it off to Dylan, who could copy and paste the correct images into the frames.

At the last, they came to a small screen-printed image, another Marilyn Monroe piece that couldn't be more different from the first one.

"Saved the best for last," Dylan said.

All pinks and oranges, it was a haphazardly collaged series of Marilyn Monroe photographs crowded together into one image, all of them depicting the same day at the beach: Marilyn frolicking in the sand in her bikini, waving a wrap—or was it seaweed?—behind her in the wind. Smiling beautifully as she came closer and closer to the camera. Except, all but one of the photographs were defaced. Some with checkmarks, one with a handwritten GOOD, but most with huge, angry Xs, often crossing out the whole of Marilyn's face on that first furious stroke.

Rob didn't get it at all.

"*My Marilyn*, by Richard Hamilton," Dylan announced, and waited for Rob to take it down in his notebook. "Marilyn Monroe liked to personally vet photographs of her. That's what the markings on the photos are, telling the photographer or her publicist or whoever which images she likes enough to publish and which ones she doesn't."

Well, that was a much more practical explanation than the graffiti or defacement Rob had first assumed, but somehow it didn't make up for the sense of anger—of the intent to *destroy*—that Rob still felt radiating in waves off those markings.

"The artist made this shortly after her death. I read about how he probably called it *My Marilyn* to separate it from the similar work Andy Warhol was doing of her at the same time." He tilted his head toward the huge wall of Marilyns at the gallery's entrance in illustration.

"Oh," Rob said, writing quickly.

"But I think there's more to it. I mean, look at Marilyn Monroe. Changed her face, her hair, her body, her name, all for us. So we'd *accept* her. A cultural icon then, a cult one now. She died in probably one of the worst and most pathetic ways a person can die, and yet there's what, three, four? generations of teenage girls who all idolize and identify with her." Rob had stopped writing, was instead watching rapt as Dylan stared into the gaudy image, his hand twitching with the held-back desire to touch it, maybe even reach through it. "So I guess what I'm saying is, you know, if the artist just wanted to make a statement in opposition to Warhol, he'd have used his name. *Hamilton's Marilyn* or something, although I guess that doesn't sound as good. But he called it *My Marilyn*, like he owned her, or a piece of her anyway, like how we all feel about celebrities and Marilyn Monroe in particular. *My Marilyn*. Our Marilyn. But then you see the markings, how many photos she kept private versus the one picture she approved of—" He pointed at the bottom left Marilyn, caught mid-laugh, seeming to dance, chin raised and collarbones in sharp definition. "And it makes you feel like you never knew her—never really *had* her at all."

Yes. Yes. Even the most public person, the most carefully composed, the most aware of their image and how they affected people, *especially* that person, had secrets nobody but a few could know, secrets that were angry and hurtful and killing them on the inside, and all the while the world comforted themselves with the sanitized version and—

Dylan was still staring at *My Marilyn*, lost in the power of the image, the power only he could see. But Rob was lost in Dylan.

No resisting this new center of gravity. He reached out, caught Dylan's soft fingers in his own clay-callused ones. Stepped close as he wove their fingers together, until their hands were clasped tight and so warm. And then he stood on his tiptoes and pressed their lips together, knowing that Dylan could easily fight him off and reject him, but he *wasn't*.

My Dylan, and simultaneously not mine at all.

CHAPTER 11

S ure, Rob had been kissed before. He wasn't *that* much of a loser.

But oh, he'd sure as hell never been kissed like this.

Dylan hadn't been expecting the kiss, but he wasn't startled by it for long. He sprang into action, grabbing Rob by the shoulders and spinning them both until Rob's back slammed against the bare white wall. Kissing him all the while, little gasps for breath sounding out of the corners of their lips as they collided and broke apart.

"Hope to hell you know what you're doing," Dylan growled, boxing Rob in with his body, looming over him, overpowering him, taking over his senses in an assault a thousand times more powerful than Warhol's Marilyns.

"I'm a big boy," Rob gasped back, staring hard into Dylan's narrowed eyes, daring him to call Rob puny now. "I think I know what I'm getting into."

No more talking. Dylan lunged forward and covered Rob's mouth with his own. Tightened his grip on Rob's shoulders the deeper his tongue got into Rob's mouth. Behind his eyelids, Rob's world erupted into neon colors, pink and teal and orange and yellow, a riot of sensation too powerful to process. Teeth on his lower lip. Dry lips sticking to his own. Tongue sweeping across his tongue. Breath puffing against his skin. A hand cupping his cheek.

A hand cupping his cheek, tilting his face upward, gently posing him like a doll. Two sides of the same masculine power—forceful strength and sweet tenderness—and Rob was captured, helpless, at the chaotic center point where they crashed together. If this kiss and this meeting were a whirlpool, then he wanted to drown in it. If they were a tornado, then he wanted to be carried away forever.

"Hey! You two!"

The vacuum they were in exploded open, the outside world rushing back toward them and carrying a security guard with it. He was waving a nightstick that he clearly didn't intend to hit anybody with, not remotely threatening or imposing, but Rob still wilted with embarrassment, half back to his senses. Dylan's kissed-red mouth just broke out in a big grin.

"Yeah, I'm talkin' to you," the guard shouted once they were both looking, and for some Godforsaken reason, Rob gaped in the opposite direction, as if there were another pair of horny dudes just behind them rutting against the collection's Lichtenstein. When he turned back to the guard again, he was stopped a few feet away, still shaking that nightstick like an ornery old man with a cane. "Yeah, you two! Not in here, you hear me? Now get!"

"Fascist!" Dylan yelled back, but he was laughing, and he grabbed Rob's hand. Tugged on it insistently as Rob stooped to pick up his fallen notebook and stuff it into his bag. He'd sacrifice the pen, wherever it was. And then he was up and they were running, dodging through the maze of white walls past a neon blur, back toward the red fire escape sign. Rob had a second or so to think how it could easily be a piece of art in this exhibit, with its hard industrial lines and bright geometry altered by its new context, and then the security guard yelled, "Not through there!" and Dylan pushed the bar anyway, and they fell together into the frigid, rainy alley to the high, aggressive chirp of the fire alarm.

The rain drenched them both in seconds, Rob's hair plastered to his face, and he thought that would be it for them, but Dylan grabbed him again and shoved him under a steel overhang where he was half sheltered from the rain and kissed him again. He wished he could say the kiss warmed him up, but it didn't; he shivered against Dylan's body, trying to find the slivers of warmth that could still penetrate the heavy ice-cold fabric of Dylan's soaking wet sweatshirt. No luck there. He let Dylan's hot breath warm his mouth instead.

He couldn't believe this was happening. He'd never been kicked out of *anywhere*, unless you counted temporary bans from 4chan. He'd definitely never kissed a guy in public, and in a filthy back alley at that. It took that romantic cliché of kissing in the rain and twisted it sideways into a bizarre mirror-world version, and Rob couldn't get enough of it.

He bucked against Dylan's big body, let out little moaning yips into Dylan's mouth. But as much as he squirmed, as hard as he pressed himself forward, Dylan's hands stayed above the waist, massaging Rob's shoulders or stroking his neck or combing through his wet hair.

Enough of this shit. Rob reached up, caught Dylan's right hand in his left one, and guided it down where it needed to go.

Dylan let himself be posed, but once his palm was cupping Rob's cock, it didn't squeeze or rub, it just held still, frozen in more than one way. Dylan pulled out of their kiss and stared down into Rob's eyes as both their panting breaths erupted in white gusts between them. "You sure about this?" Dylan asked, voice steady, but Rob could hear the harsh need there too, suppressed but present.

"Yeah. As long as you are."

A gentle squeeze, then, as Dylan massaged Rob's aching shaft through the tight denim of his jeans. "This is okay? Me touching you here? Like this?"

"For fuck's sake, of course it is. It better be, since I put your hand there in the first place. Now, c'mon, you dragged me out into this sketchy back alley, so you better give me the whole experience."

"Be careful what you wish for," Dylan warned, eyes twinkling, and lowered himself to his knees.

"Oh!" Rob cried, falling against the cement wall of the gallery. "Oh, oh shit, I didn't mean that! You don't have to—"

"Do you want it? Because if you want it, I want it." He palmed Rob's dick, teasing him with not nearly enough pressure. And then the bastard licked his lips. Looking down and seeing Dylan looking up, it was like the whole world had tilted on its side. *Poseidon Adventure: Blowjob Edition.*

"Yeah, God yeah, I want it, but in this rain your knees you'll get wet and holy shit holy holy holy—"

Dylan had opened his fly. Had pulled his bare, hot cock out through the Y of his briefs and into the cool air. "Love that poem," Dylan said as Rob gibbered past comprehension and gave himself over to the feeling of those soft but powerful hands wrapped around his shaft, shielding it from the cold and twisting sinfully in opposite directions. Wringing him out.

Anyone could see. Anyone could walk by. There might be surveillance cameras. Rob must have been going crazy. What poem was Dylan even talking about? He shouted and hissed as Dylan's hot, wet mouth took in the head of his cock. He clawed at the wall for purchase as Dylan's flexible tongue lapped at his pre-cum-drenched slit. And the whole while, those two hands locked around his shaft like a vice, twisting and twisting and twisting, driving him fucking wild while Dylan expertly worked the head.

Who needed deep-throating when you could have this?

He kept his hands on the wall, didn't dare touch Dylan's head, didn't want to disturb his flow or his groove or whatever. And anyway, he was happy being passive, happy letting Dylan *do* things to him. And God were they amazing things. Mind-blowing things. Ball- and toe-tingling things. Oh. *Oh.*

"Shit, I'm gonna—" He tried to rear back, but one of Dylan's powerful hands snaked around behind him, grabbing a handful of his ass and keeping him close, no, not just keeping him close, pulling him in, drawing him forward until he was fucking into Dylan's throat. And even though Dylan was gagging, he wasn't letting Rob pull away; he just held him tight until he arched and shot, until the mind-bending *My Marilyn* pink that washed over him faded back into the glittering blackness of the wet alley again.

"*Nice*," Dylan croaked like a man who'd just taken a hit off a bong, and sat back on his heels to put Rob's dick away again and zip him up. He wiped a rope of drool from his chin with the cuff of his sweatshirt.

"That was—" Rob sputtered. "Do you want me to—" His knees buckled.

Dylan was on his feet in an instant, catching Rob before he slumped right onto his ass in a puddle. He held him in a bear hug, and Rob shivered down to his bones, teeth suddenly chattering, his clothes sopping wet and ice cold. "Don't worry about it, Puny. What do you weigh, eighty pounds? We better get you out of this rain before you freeze to death."

"A h-h-hundred and t-twenty," Rob stuttered, dazed as Dylan threw an arm around his back and half carried him out of the alley and into the gallery parking lot.

"Shit!" Dylan shouted, and Rob looked up from his drunken two left feet just in time to see the bus fly by. "Won't be another one for at least a half an hour, this time of the night. Shit, shit." He reached into his front kangaroo pocket and pulled out a battered cell phone.

"What are y-you—"

"Calling you a cab, Puny, before you get hypothermia or pneumonia or something." He keyed in the numbers and raised his phone to his ear, and Rob watched him, a little bit stunned, as he ordered the cab.

They waited for it together in the bus shelter, sitting huddled on the bench and watching in somewhat awkward silence as the cars flew by. When Rob's cab pulled up to the curb, Dylan helped him to his feet and pressed a fifty-dollar bill into his hands. "This should get you home," he said, a little stiffly.

"N-no. No. I can't take this, Dylan. Thanks, but I'll just use my dad's Visa."

"No way. My treat. Least I can do, after subjecting you to the elements." There was no wry smile, no twinkle in his eyes.

Rob's heart pounded, and he forced himself to look at Dylan straight on, fighting back that old survival instinct to hide behind his bangs. "Come with me, then. My roommates won't mind," he pleaded, and when Dylan's impassive face didn't shift, added, "Please? We can . . . warm each other up." Too bad he missed the flirtatious mark by at least fifty miles.

Dylan shook his head and practically dumped Rob into the backseat of the cab. "I really better not. Now get going. Don't forget to have those PowerPoints to me by Friday night so I can finish everything up over the weekend."

"Oh. Um. Yeah, of course. Okay. See ya, Dylan."

"Bye, Puny."

The cab door slammed shut.

"You did *what* last night?" Bernice shrieked.

Rob stared down at the white lid of his Starbucks and pursed his lips, trying to ignore the heat of his cheeks.

And then, because either his embarrassment wasn't apparent to her or she just was too excited to care, she added "In an *alley?*"

"C'mon, Bernie, keep it down. I don't think the barista needs to know about my sex life." He snuck a look at the girl behind the counter, but she wasn't watching him too closely. He hoped it was because the whoosh of the steamer had drowned out his words, but more likely she was just used to pretending she didn't hear awkward conversations from her customers.

Damn, ever since Rear Entrance Video, he couldn't look at people in service jobs the same way.

"Wow," Bernice said, and leaned back in her seat, practically tilting it onto its back legs. She took a loud sip on the straw of her no-whip strawberry frappuccino, scrutinizing him through scrunched up eyes. "And this was with your new boyfriend? I mean, I hope it was!"

"Uh . . ." Rob said, not sure how to answer that. "About that . . ."

"Oh my God, Rob! Oh my God! You didn't! Oh my God!"

"It's not that!" Rob protested, face as hot as a furnace now. "Jeez, I come out and suddenly my sister thinks I'm doing the whole 1970s-gloryhole no-condoms thing, high off my mind on poppers . . ."

"What are poppers?"

"Ugh, don't ask. Look, what I mean is, I don't know if Dylan is my boyfriend or not. I kinda lied to you last week. Well, not about being gay, but about having a boyfriend. Sorry. I just . . . needed an excuse to leave, you know?"

Bernice pouted, pretty brow furrowed, and stabbed her frappuccino with her straw. "Well, that was shitty of you."

"Yeah, I know. I really am sorry, I'm just . . . I'm going through a weird time in my life right now."

"You're safe, right?" She reached out and clasped his hand tightly, peering into his eyes as if she could see the truth there. She probably could.

"Yes, Bernice. I am. Well, except for this cold." He sniffled for effect and took a sip of his chamomile tea.

"Well, that's good." She gave him a judgmental look for a second longer, eyelids low, body language closed off, and then a switch flipped inside her and she sat forward again, eyes sparkling. Rob wished he could ask her how she got her eyelashes like that. She seemed to have a way better handle on her mascara than he did. "So? Are you going to tell me about this guy Dylan, or what?"

"Will you forgive me if I do?" He batted his eyelashes at her.

She *tsked*. "You know you're forgiven already. But sure. Now dish."

"He's, um . . . he's in school with me. Older than me—oh my God, would you lose the scandalized look, he's not even twenty-five, okay?—and he does indie comics. I don't know, he's cute and I like him and I can actually *talk* to him and I guess maybe he likes me back? Or maybe not. After, um, the thing we did in the alley, he got all weird. Sent me home alone, wouldn't come even after I invited him."

"Robert Ng inviting a guy home. Never thought I'd see the day."

"Ha-ha. So he sends me home, but he pays my cab bill, even though it cost like forty-six bucks. Maybe he felt guilty."

"Or maybe he likes you." She smiled, giving him a sly look out of the corners of her perfect eyes.

"I don't know. He just seemed weird about the whole thing. Kept warning me off him and asking if I was *sure*."

"What is he, a Cullen? A drug dealer?"

"Who knows. I have a feeling I'm in over my head, though."

"Rob, honey, don't take this the wrong way, but you'd be in over your head if you were dating a kindergarten teacher driving a Prius."

"Thanks for the vote of confidence," Rob grumbled, but couldn't help smiling. He was glad he was talking to Bernice again. He'd missed her this past week. He only wished he could be as open about the secret at the bottom of his bag as he was about his hookup with Dylan. "Anyway, I better get to work."

She threw her cell phone into her purse and rearranged the big peachy-orange scarf she was wearing around her slim neck. "I can't believe you're working. You know Mom and Dad are paying your way specifically so you *don't* have to work and you can just focus on your schooling, right?"

Rob paid a little too much attention to zipping up his hoodie. "It's art school, Bernice. It's not like I'm doing pre-med or something."

"God, can you imagine?" she laughed.

"And anyway, I'm doing it as a favor for my roommate. It's his aunt's store and she's in treatment for cancer, so he's managing it for her while she's off work, and he's having a hard time finding reliable staff."

"You're a saint," Bernice said as they stood, and she grabbed him under one arm and kissed him square on the cheek. "Except for screening my calls all week. Don't do that again, you little shit, or else I'm telling Mom and Dad you're doing it in dirty back alleys."

Rob glowered at her. "Don't you *dare*."

"Kidding! Kidding!" And with that, she danced away from him, floating out of the shop and into the watery daylight like the frappuccino fairy.

He sighed, watching her go. Even though it hadn't really resolved anything, talking to her about Dylan had really helped with the horrible swirl of conflicting feelings inside of him. Now, if only he could calm the similarly chaotic mess about his gender confusion . . . Namely, why, for the first time in ages, had he been able to get off without falling into that girl body fantasy? Could being with Dylan *fix* him?

There's nothing to fix, he told himself as he finally left the shop.

But if that was the case, if wanting to be a girl sometimes was an inherent part of him that didn't need changing, that maybe *couldn't* be changed, then was pursuing Dylan even a good idea in the first place? It'd have to come out sometime. Maybe that blowjob had been new and novel enough that Rob hadn't needed to fall back on the fantasy, but that didn't mean it would always be like that. Bobby wasn't about to vanish out of existence forever, never to return. In fact, Rob was intending to put on the glasses and hair extensions again in less than an hour. Looking forward to it, in fact.

And if he couldn't even tell his sister—the one person in his life he knew without a doubt would always love and forgive him—about his double life, then how the hell could he ever tell Dylan? He'd always be living a lie. Living in fear of being found out, of how Dylan might react. Sure, he seemed cool now, but even the most progressive, PC people in the world still couldn't wrap their stubborn minds around people who fucked around with gender lines. Hell, even if Dylan didn't get violent, even if he kept his judgments to himself, would Rob be able to handle a rejection—even a kind one—once he'd gotten invested? Once he'd . . . fallen?

Yeah. Maybe Dylan pushing him away was for the best after all. Too bad Rob's heart didn't agree.

CHAPTER 12

I n the end, Bobby wound up lasting roughly half his shift before he had to call Max and beg for mercy.

"Max," he croaked into the phone in his Rob voice, not that this cold was really conducive to doing his Bobby one properly, "Max, please please please, you gotta come take this shift, I think I'm dying."

Okay, probably not, but he was leaking snot like a faucet and coughing like he had consumption. Even Charlie VIP had kept his distance. All Bobby wanted to do was get these hair extensions out, wash this makeup off, get out of this itchy fucking bra, and climb into bed, where he could sleep for thirty hours straight.

"Aw, Rob, seriously, man?" Max complained. On the other end of the phone, Bobby could hear a murmur in the background. Probably Christian. "It's Rob. Yeah. Little nugget says he's sick. Yeah. Yeah. Oh, *fine*—hey, Rob, I'm back. Okay, Christian says if I don't come in he's not gonna give me blowjobs for a week, so I guess you've got a replacement. Give me an hour?"

"Sure." Bobby sneezed. Sniffled. "Sure, sure. See you soon. Tell Christian thank you."

"What about *my* thank you?"

"Oh, fine. Thanks for giving in to Christian's blackmail, Max."

"You're welcome," Max said with an imperious sniff, and hung up.

And thank God the phone call ended when it did, because not a second later, the bell over the door jingled.

"Welcome to Rear Entrance Video," Bobby said, dabbing at his nose with a tissue.

In walked Adam Fickes in his Hollister cap. "You don't look too good, babydoll," he said, flopping over the counter and holding out his rental disc.

"Yeah, I got caught out in the rain last night." As sick as Bobby was, a warm feeling pooled in his lower belly, remembering—until, of course, the ice-cold shock of remembering what had happened after hit.

Dylan, sending him home alone.

He took the case from Adam's hand and scanned it, refusing to look the guy in the eye as he processed the return.

"So gettin' caught in the rain . . . is that why you didn't call me, baby?"

Ugh, please don't make me have this conversation.

"Sorry, I guess I should have just told you up front we're not allowed to date customers."

"Whaaat!" Adam snapped his fingers in frustration. "Seriously? What's your boss care who you date?"

Bobby shrugged. "I don't make the rules, I just follow them."

Now, please get out of my face so I can close up shop and de-girl before Max shows up here and gets a fun surprise.

"Okay, okay, well how about this. How about when your shift's over, I just happen to be standing outside waiting for a bus, and I just happen to see you walking by and ask you for your digits. Not your customer then, am I?"

"I don't know . . ." Bobby mumbled, ducking his head in just the right way to cause his hair to curtain half his face. He sniffled again. "I'm honestly just waiting for my coworker to come take over for me, and then I'm going straight home to bed."

Why the hell don't you just say no? So much for Bobby being able to say and do all the things Rob was too chicken to. But then, maybe Bobby's powers were weakened by *Walking Dead* levels of illness. You could hardly blame the girl.

"I get it, I get it. I know when I'm not wanted. What, you got a boyfriend, is that it?"

Yes, tell him yes. "Yeah. I do. I don't normally talk about him here, but yeah, I do."

The bruises on Adam's ego seemed to heal, because the macho hurt went from his voice. "He Asian like you? Because let me tell you, if you're dating an Asian guy, you are *missing out.*"

"Um . . ." Bobby examined his nails, for lack of anything else to look at.

"Bet you my dick's twice as big as his." Bobby must have given him a shocked look at that, because he put up both hands in a pitch-perfect white Kanye impression. "Just sayin.'"

"Okay, well, that's good, but I really need to get back to work now." And then, for good measure, Bobby hacked out a nasty, wet cough into his hands.

That did the trick. Adam finally retreated, walking backward toward the door, but he couldn't help one last attempt just before he slipped out. "Get better soon, babe. You think over that bus stop offer. Think of me when you're rubbing the Vicks on your tits tonight. Nine inches!"

Yeah. Sure.

As soon as the bell jingled, Bobby rushed to the door and locked it behind him, breathing a sigh of relief at the click.

Forty minutes later when Max sauntered in, it was Rob waiting for him behind the counter.

Days passed. Rob got sicker. By Thursday, he was completely bedridden.

Friday afternoon, he was woken by a text.

Send me ur house address. Bringing u the week's homework b/c dr chasTITTY can't do email. Typical prof. Also need notes for those powerpoints I assume u never got around to making.

Dylan. He sounded pissed.

Well, fair enough. It was obvious the guy had been burned in group projects before, judging by the fact that he'd wanted to get to the gallery before Rob had had a chance to procrastinate or get slippery on the dates. And now here it was, Friday, and Rob was flaking on his half of the assignment. Sure, he was sick, but too sick to get his ass to his computer? If he was in Dylan's position, he'd be *furious*. After all, Dylan was doing him a favor by doing the presentation solo in exchange for the PowerPoint notes.

Rob texted back his address, along with a simple note: *Sorry.*

As if things weren't awkward enough already.

He flopped back onto his pillow, one-hundred percent intending to get up, get dressed, and tidy up a bit, maybe at least type up his notes so Dylan could just copy-paste them onto the PowerPoint . . . and promptly fell asleep.

A knock at his door jolted him awake again.

Noah, probably. The guy had been forcing hot and spicy soups on him for days, saying they'd "clear out his sinuses."

"Whatever it is, Noah, thanks, but no thanks! My poor sick taste buds need a break!"

"It's not Noah," Dylan's voice sounded through the door.

Fuck! What time was it? He sat up and rubbed his eyes. Peered at his alarm clock. Five in the evening, seriously? *Shitshitshit.*

"Coming! Coming! Sorry sorry . . ." He rolled out of bed—literally, rolled right onto the floor with a crash, then had to use the mattress to lever himself to his feet. Okay, no time to get dressed, but the least he could do was put on a T-shirt. He stumbled across his room, pinballing off walls and furniture and listing like a drunk. Finally he made it to his dresser, where he ransacked his drawers until he found a shirt he wasn't embarrassed to be seen in: his PE T-shirt from high school. He pulled it over his head, got his arms in the sleeves, and dove for the door.

"Finally," Dylan said as soon as he opened the door, and forced his way into the room like he owned the place. "Your fucking roommate's shirtless and flexing his muscles at himself in the bathroom mirror with the door open." He mimicked gagging himself with a finger.

"That would be Austin. I think his head is literally made of meat. Um, come in, make yourself at . . . home?"

Dylan obviously didn't need an invitation, because he was already sprawled out on Rob's bed. He had an overstuffed black Dickies book bag between his legs on the floor and an unmarked paper bag on his lap. Maybe he'd picked himself up some supper on his way.

"This is for you," he said, and held out the bag.

Or he was way more of a gentleman than Rob had given him credit for. Wow.

"Uh, thanks, wow. You didn't have to do that. Really. Shit."

"Yeah I did. It's my fault you're sick, after all."

"Um, that's not really how viruses work, but thanks all the same." The heat in Rob's cheeks definitely wasn't the low-grade fever he'd been fighting the last few days. He unrolled the top of the bag and sat. There was a take-out bowl and a plastic spoon inside. "Chicken noodle soup?" he asked.

"How basic do you think I am?" Dylan said, laying on the offense thick. "Open it."

Rob did, and the minute the smell of the steam hit his nostrils, he felt his chest swell with the deepest, basest gratitude there was. "Is this . . . is this congee?"

Dylan nodded with a grin. "You like it? I had to go to this restaurant where the old woman running the counter didn't speak English to get it, but luckily there was someone our age in line with me and she translated."

"Mmm, do I like it? I love it. When I'm sick, at least. Wow, thank you." For the first time in days, his slumbering appetite stirred. Sure, the food was bland, the exact opposite of what Noah thought he should eat to get his hunger back, but there was no beating it on a primal comfort level. He dug in, not even the remotest bit self-conscious at the way Dylan was staring at him with a dopey smile the entire time.

"Good," Dylan said. "You know, I missed you this week. Which is kinda crazy since we don't really know each other all that well—"

"You know me well enough to bring me congee when I'm sick."

"Don't take this the wrong way, Puny, but you're not my first Chinese boyfriend."

Rob nearly spat out his mouthful of congee. "What?"

Dylan laughed and rubbed the back of his neck. "Oh, yeah, I dated this guy William Chan in tenth? No, eleventh grade. He was *way* high maintenance. And superattached to his mom. Creepy attached. Probably still shares a bed with her on stormy nights."

"No, the other part." *The part about me being your boyfriend, you colossal idiot.*

"Oh! Boyfriend! Well, uh, I mean, if you want to. If being with me is what you really, *really* want."

Why did he say it like that, like being boyfriends was some huge decision or commitment? Did he not want Rob to say yes to him? Then why bring it up at all? Rob frowned as the cold, awkward reality set in. Sure, Dylan had called him his boyfriend, but he'd also ditched him that night at the gallery without an explanation. An explanation that Rob damn well deserved. "I do want that, but not until you tell me . . ." He stirred the congee counterclockwise. "Why did you run out on me the other night? Doesn't seem very *boyfriend*-y."

Dylan had the good sense to look chastened. "You're right. It wasn't. I got cold feet, I guess. You're just so . . . I don't know, cute and innocent with your baby face. And getting asked home like that, after the coffee and everything, it didn't freak me out, exactly, but I was worried that maybe you didn't understand what you were really asking for."

What I was really asking for? "Sex, Dylan. I was asking for sex. That's why I invited you home. You don't have to be so . . ." He groaned, struggle to come up with the words. "Protective of me. I know I'm younger than you, but I'm not a little kid. I can make my own decisions. I know you mean well, but how about you let *me* do the worrying about what I want?"

"Right," Dylan said, and now he was definitely looking ashamed, his head ducked between his shoulders like Rob was taking away his TV privileges. "Of course. Sorry."

"But we could give it a try," Rob added shyly. He stared down into his bowl, suddenly unable to even look at Dylan.

"Yeah. A try." Dylan's voice was optimistic, and he slapped his hands on his thighs. "Nothing too serious. Anything . . . comes up, we end it. No harm, no foul. Okay."

Well, that was a little cold-blooded. *But I'll take it.* "Okay," Rob said, trying to keep his voice peppy. "Deal. Boyfriends." He held out his hand, and Dylan looked down at it, and then back up at Rob's face like he'd grown a second head.

"You want to *shake on it?*"

"Oh! Uh." Rob withdrew his hand.

Instead, Dylan leaned forward, cupped Rob's nape to gather him in, and pressed a gentle kiss to his forehead.

Happy sigh.

"All done with this, Puny?" Dylan's hand covered Rob's holding the bowl.

Yes, yes, he was. In fact . . . Rob slumped sideways, quite suddenly unable to remain upright. Luckily, Dylan got the half-finished bowl of congee out of his hands before it had a chance to spill. He set the bowl aside, and then turned to tuck Rob in, gently smoothing the blankets over his chest.

"You need anything else? Meds?"

"Nuh," Rob slurred, eyelids drooping.

"Okay, you just let me know, then." With that, Dylan stripped his sweatshirt, leaving him barebacked, and then stood to shuck himself out of his jeans.

"Whu ya doin'?" Rob fought off the bizarre urge to avert his eyes.

"Getting under the covers?" Dylan replied. And so he did. Climbed into the bed beside Rob, elbowing him over a few inches, and then settled back using his upper arm as a pillow. "I assume the offer to stay the night is still open?"

"Yeah," Rob said. "But it's not night."

"If you must know my itinerary, I plan to snuggle until you fall asleep, then snoop through your shit—kidding, I'm kidding!—and then get this project typed up. Where are your notes, by the way? Otherwise I *will* have to snoop."

"Desk. Composition notebook."

"Composition notebook," Dylan mimicked with a derisive snort. He shook his head. "Fucking hipster."

Rob was asleep again before he could reply.

Rob woke up the next morning to two very pleasant surprises: one, that he could breathe out of his nose for the first time in days, and two, that Dylan was still in bed with him, his big body spooned up against Rob's back.

Okay, make that three very pleasant surprises. The third, of course, being the wonderful, thick erection nudging Rob's ass.

"Mmm." He wiggled in Dylan's arms and not-so-subtly pressed that erection closer. "*Good* morning."

Dylan chuckled into his hair. "Is it, now? My congee work its magic?"

"Either that, or you snuck me some heavy duty cough syrup while I was out."

"I would never." A big palm caressed Rob's flat belly and slipped downward, gently cupping his growing cock. "This okay?"

That woke Rob up the rest of the way, from sleepy-slack to totally tense in a matter of seconds. "Yes, for God's sake. Do you need it in writing or something?" He cleared his throat and spoke in a stuffy, official voice: "This is to state that the undersigned, Rob Ng, gives Dylan Ford permission to manhandle his dick in perpetuity."

"Smartass."

"My sister's in pre-law."

"And do you normally invoke her in matters of the boner?"

Rob twisted around until they were face to face. He gave Dylan his very best *I'm being serious* look. "If it gets you to stop treating me like your very own *No Means No* PSA. Because, dude, I'm all for enthusiastic consent, but it's pretty weird when every time you ask, you make it sound like I should be saying no."

Dylan's brow crumpled, his eyes glancing away, avoiding Rob's stare. "Sorry."

"Don't be." Rob took him by the chin and pressed their lips together in a quick, but he hoped meaningful, kiss. "I mean, here I am ragging on my boyfriend for being *too considerate*. Sounds like the only person who needs to apologize here is me."

That perked Dylan up, because his chastened expression broke into a big lecherous grin. "Well, in that case . . . I dunno about an apology exactly, but I sure do have a few ideas on how you can make it up to me."

"Oh?" Rob cooed back, giving a girly little one-shouldered-shrug-and-head-tilt combo. "I hope some of them include your dick inside me."

Dylan gulped, eyes going wide. "Uh," he said.

"I think you'll find you mean 'Uh-huh,'" Rob replied with a wink. He'd *never* seen Dylan speechless before, and, to be honest, he kinda liked it. Not the speechless part, necessarily—because he loved hearing Dylan talk, loved the things he said and the totally unabashed way he said them—but the part where Rob had the power to make that smart mouth speechless? Hell, yeah, he liked that.

He didn't know what was going to come of their relationship, exactly, especially considering Dylan's plain-stated timidity about commitment, but he knew that for as long as it lasted, Rob would be on a never-ending quest to make Dylan speechless.

Starting now.

Before Dylan could find his voice again, Rob gave him a peck on the chin and shimmied down under the covers.

Hot under here, and Dylan's masculine scent filled Rob's senses.

Heady, that was the word, and oh yes, so appropriate. Rob rucked up Dylan's soft red T-shirt, exposing his soft, almost smooth belly. Kissed him there, loving the give of Dylan's flesh under his lips. Cupped Dylan's hips in his hands and pressed his whole face in, kissing him, breathing him in, nosing the soft near invisible hair under his belly button. Dylan didn't touch him, didn't push him down, just kept his hands fisted in Rob's sheets, so tight they were white-knuckled.

Rob lifted his head. "You can touch me," he said. "Mister Needs-Permission."

Outside the blankets, Dylan laughed, and his whole body shook, exposed belly jiggling a little with the force of it. "Forget Thomas Builds-the-Fire. Make way for Dylan Needs-Permission," he said.

Rob flicked him in the side. "Shhh," he said. "Unless you're dirty-talking."

"Dirty talk, huh? Okay, how about this." The blanket flew off Rob's head, exposing him to the cold air of the room and dissipating Dylan's intoxicating scent into the air. "Get rid of that blanket so I can watch your pretty face when you suck me off."

Pretty, he called me pretty. Rob's bones wanted to melt, but he had a job to do. So he looked up Dylan's body—he'd propped himself up on a pillow and was now looking down on Rob with one arm tucked lazily under his head—and gave him a slow lick of his lips.

"Mmm," Dylan said, and reached down with his free arm to press the pad of his thumb to Rob's lower lip, tugging it down until Rob could feel his fingerprint on the wet inside of his lip and the bottoms of his lower teeth. Not breaking eye contact, Rob opened his mouth and drew that thumb in. Drew *Dylan* in, body and spirit, capturing his thumb and his attention. He sucked gently, tasting familiar salt. The whole time, Dylan watched him, eyes dark, lower lip caught in his teeth. At last, he found his voice to speak. "That's not my dick, you know."

Rob freed Dylan's thumb with one last lick. "You're the one who put it in my mouth."

"Allow me to rectify the situation, then." Dylan used his spit-wet thumb to hook the waistband of his boxers and pull them down. His cock sprang free in all its magnificent uncut glory, thick and hooded with a pair of tight, dark balls at its base. Practically hairless, except for a neat, dense bush. Rob watched, salivating, as Dylan jacked himself with just his thumb and forefinger. Watched that meaty foreskin slide up and down, revealing the tiniest sliver of deep purple crown. And then he pressed that mouthwatering monster to Rob's lips, just as he'd done with his thumb.

And just as Rob had done with Dylan's thumb, he caught and held Dylan's gaze and drew the offered member into his mouth with a cheeky smile. Sucked briefly, and then—*pop!*—let it slip out again. Dylan grunted in frustration. Rob was having too much fun teasing to stop, though. Keeping his hands to himself, he caught that dick in his mouth over and over again, alternating hard, vigorous sucks with light, cruel ones. Dylan tossed his head on Rob's pillow, bit his lip some more, but didn't speak. He really was *too* considerate. Damn but Rob fell a little in love with him for that.

Time to take pity on the guy. Rob swept his hair behind one ear and took the very tip of Dylan's dick in his mouth once more, but this time, rather than the suck-and-release game, he forced his head down, down, down, to take at least half of that huge shaft into his mouth. The slippery, taut head bumped the insides of his cheek, and then down it went, hitting his gag reflex hard and then barrelling right past it. Rob loved it, loved taking a man deep and feeling him squirm. It made him feel sexy, powerful, and the drool on his chin was pornographic and oh-so-good.

"Jesus fucking Christ!" Dylan roared, trying to sit up, abs visibly clenching under that soft outer layer, but then he fell back again as Rob pulled off him. His big dick was coated in a thick glaze of Rob's spit, and Rob used it to jerk him off while the fingers of his opposite hand tickled down Dylan's taint and back to pet his tightly furled hole.

"You ever bottom?" Rob asked conversationally, prodding just the tip of his middle finger into that clenching ass.

Dylan didn't reply right away. Rob wasn't sure he could, the way he was panting. A hot, red flush covered him from neck to nipples. Sexy. "You wanna top?" Dylan finally managed to grit out, his voice rough.

As a rule, Rob actually preferred to bottom, but if he wanted to keep Bobby at bay, he thought that a little unwise. Which was fucked up, considering his previous determination not to change that part of himself, not even for Dylan. Oh well, he could kick himself over it later. Right now, he had an ass to fuck. "If that's okay with youuu," he finally replied, in a way-too-whiny imitation of Dylan's own words.

"Hell, yeah, it is, you little fucking smartass." But despite the peevishness of his tone, Dylan still laughed. "How do you want me, then?"

Good question. "What do you like? And do you have a condom?"

Dylan kicked out of his boxers and hooked his hands under his knees, hitching them up to his shoulders in a silent-but-meaningful reply to Rob's question, but he promptly dropped them again. "What? Please tell me I was just hearing you wrong when you said you don't have condoms."

"Uh, no, sorry? I haven't gotten laid in a while, to be honest." Between his shyness and lack of human interaction, never mind the incomprehensible tangle that was his gender identity/presentation, he hadn't really gotten a lot of opportunities.

"Shit! I was counting on you there, Puny! Because I sure as hell don't."

"You don't?" Rob's mouth fell open. "You came over here without them?"

"Yeah, well, you were sick, remember? I'm not a sleaze."

Rob's aching dick dropped to half-mast. He puffed up his cheeks, then let out the breath in a huff. "Okay. Okay. Well, house of guys, right? One of 'em's bound to. Give me a sec." He got up, wrapped his duvet around his body to hide what was left of his erection, and steeled himself for the awkwardness to come.

CHAPTER 13

First stop, Christian's (and unofficially Max's) room. Rob took a deep breath and knocked lightly.

"Go the fuck away!" Max shouted through the door, and it sounded like Christian was trying to say something else, but whatever it might have been was clearly being smothered by a palm. Oh, and there it was, the telltale slap of flesh on flesh.

Okay, there went the safest avenue.

Which left . . . Noah or Austin.

Yikes. Maybe Rob would be better off going back to Dylan empty-handed and they could sixty-nine or jack each other off instead.

Don't be a fucking coward. After all, Dylan was worth being brave—and majorly embarrassed—for.

Okay, so Noah, or Austin?

Noah's "room" was in the converted attic, so Austin was closer. But Austin was kind of a dick.

On the other hand, while he and Noah were on much better terms, he wasn't sure if their newfound lack of awkwardness would extend to matters of sex. And what if his girlfriend was with him?

Austin it was. Rob strode up to his door, took another deep breath.

And then another. *Okay. Okay. Okay.*

He knocked.

"Come in!" Austin called.

So far so good. Better than his reception from Max had been, at least.

Rob opened the door and poked his head in. Austin was sitting on his computer chair in his boxers and a wifebeater, puffing and red-faced as he did bicep curls with hand weights. His sweaty muscles bulged, and Rob half forgot himself.

Dylan. His boyfriend. His *boyfriend*.

"Hey Austin," he said with feeble wave.

"'Sup," Austin replied, still lifting.

"I was just wondering if I could ask you for a, um, a favor. Maybe. Possibly." His face felt as hot as a tea kettle. Maybe he'd start whistling soon.

"Sure. C'mon, spit it out and let me get back to my reps."

"I kinda, I, well, that is, doyouhaveacondom?"

"A what?" Austin's big blue All-American (Canadian?) eyes bugged out.

C'mon man, you fucking heard me. Don't make this worse than it is.
"A condom. A rubber."

"What the hell you need one of those for? You doing some kind of art . . . thing?"

Rob rolled his eyes. "Sex, Austin. I need one for sex. So do you have one or not?"

Austin dropped his weights and pulled a face. "Gross, man, I didn't want to know that!" *Then why the fuck did you ask?* "What, with that guy who came to see you yesterday? Jesus, are all my roommates fuckin' gay?"

"It appears so," Rob snapped. "So better wear a face mask from now on. It may be catching."

"Ugh, don't say that." Austin did a fake shudder, but he did stand and go for his bedside drawer, tossing a whole strip of condoms Rob's way. Extra large size, of course. What a meathead. "Here. Take them all. Don't want you coming here when you go for round two or whatever. And please don't tell me who's wearing them."

Rob wouldn't have dreamed of telling Austin that under normal circumstances, but that was the last straw as far as this conversation was concerned. "*I* am, Austin. I am going to fuck my boyfriend's ass wearing your overcompensation condom. Better put on some headphones."

And with that, he turned on his heel, savoring the look of horror on Austin's stupid meathead face.

I am going to fuck my boyfriend. His chest puffed out in pride. *I am all man, and I am going to use my dick to fuck my boyfriend.*

He was rock hard in his boxers by the time he got back to his room. After how long it had taken to acquire condoms, he'd kind of expected to find Dylan snooping around impatient or fully dressed and ready to bolt, but instead he found the man sprawled out on his bed, naked and debauched and—oh good fucking God—fingering his own hole with two thick fingers while he jerked himself with the opposite hand.

"Found your lube," he said once Rob had walked in and shut the door behind him. "Hope you don't mind I went in your bedside drawer. I like your dildo."

Rob blushed fiercely, but forced himself to own it. *I am going to fuck my boyfriend,* he repeated to himself. "Thanks, I like it too. A lot. Maybe sometime you and he can get acquainted."

"Hmm, I think it's a little early in our relationship to be suggesting threesomes, don't you?"

"Too soon? Never," Rob replied with a feral grin, and threw the duvet from his shoulders. Oh yes, he was going to fuck that ready, willing ass. He peeled off his T-shirt and boxers, tore open one of Austin's condoms, rolled it down his dick, and threw the rest of the strip over his shoulder. Climbed onto the bed, right on top of Dylan, and gave him a deep, hard kiss.

"Damn," Dylan said once they'd broken apart again. Rob grabbed his smooth legs and pushed them up again, letting Dylan hold them in place. Dylan's slippery brown hole came into view and Rob's cock jerked impatiently. "You don't waste time, do you, Puny?"

"Chinese," Rob said, his voice clipped. He took the base of his cock in hand and rubbed the sheathed head against that hungry hole. It twitched, opening a little in greeting. "Very efficient."

"Efficient meets Indian Time," Dylan said, looking him in the eyes, and in that moment he was strangely beautiful, the flat planes of his face so open and honest.

"Thought you were Inuit," Rob joked.

"Eh, without the mukluks and those bone goggle things, who even knows the fuckin' difference anymore?"

Rob tilted his head, one hand still on his cock and the other resting on Dylan's softly rising ribcage. Time seemed to stop. "You do," he said.

Dylan blinked, and his eyes seemed wet and shiny, but then he smiled a jagged smile, all teeth. "Come on and fuck me then, my efficient artist."

"Yeah," Rob breathed back, and pushed forward, so slow. The tightness, the heat of Dylan's body, the slightly pained expression on Dylan's face, all combined to nearly knock the breath out of him.

"That's good. Damn. That's good. That's good." Dylan threw his head back, fingers digging hard into his own thighs.

Rob stroked Dylan's tense fingers. "Wrap your legs around me," he instructed, and Dylan did, his ankles hooking in the dip of Rob's lower back, his hands stroking Rob's shoulder blades and up to tangle in the long hair at Rob's nape. Pressed close like this, Rob could feel Dylan's cock rubbing against his stomach, could feel Dylan's wet breath on his shoulder as he began to pump his hips and Dylan began to pant.

Hard, slow, *deep* fucking. That was what Rob liked, not that frantic jackhammering he'd heard going on in Christian and Max's room. Truth was, he wasn't efficient at all. He liked taking his time, liked to really feel his dick sliding up that tight channel, liked watching those slow shifts of expression on Dylan's face as the angle and depth changed. It was like watching time-lapse photography of clouds passing overhead, a perfect, beautiful shift. Dylan's eyebrows. His fluttering eyelids. His tightening jaw. His expressive mouth and Hollywood-white teeth. Even his nostrils flaring. Rob loved it all, loved controlling it, loved the sweet, undeniable magic of knowing someone else so intimately.

This wasn't the Dylan who joked awkwardly with him at Rear Entrance Video, wasn't the Dylan who kicked his feet up on his desk at school. This was Dylan stripped down to just his body, a Dylan that Rob could imagine was his alone. Not really, and he didn't expect that or even want it, but for now, in this moment, their bodies locked together, the illusion was intoxicating and overpowering and all-encompassing. Alpha and the Omega biblical shit.

Yeah, Rob was a man, all right. No doubt about it. He pumped harder, picked up the pace chasing his orgasm. Dylan was jerking himself off now, punching Rob in the gut with every flick of his wrist. Rob didn't mind. The strikes were like a metronome dictating his pace, letting him match the rhythm Dylan most needed in that moment. And Dylan's ass was tightening around him, milking him—muscles that contracted starting at the base of his dick and rippled upward, all the way up his shaft until they squeezed his head, God. Rob's eyes rolled back in his head and he let out a hoarse cry, absurdly hoping in that moment that Austin had taken his suggestion of headphones to heart.

Fuck it, who cared. Let them all hear. Rob was a man. Rob was a man. Rob was a man.

They came together, kissing and moaning into each other's mouths, wet, broken sounds that matched the desperate slapping of Rob's dick in Dylan's tight, lubed hole, slowing now.

Rob shivered all over, body giving out, and when he collapsed it was a soft landing, his small, bony body perfectly fitting against Dylan's bigger, fleshier one. So small, so delicate, especially when Dylan swept his long bangs back out of his eyes and kissed his sweaty forehead, then rubbed their noses together.

"Eskimo kiss," Rob said with a mindless giggle, then felt sorry for it.

"*Kunik*," Dylan corrected, no offense in his tone. "But that's not one." He pressed their faces close, nudging his nose below Rob's cheekbone and inhaling deep enough that he drew Rob's skin to his using just his breath. "*That* is. Because I think I'm starting to love you."

You confusing, contradictory idiot.

I think I'm starting to love you, too.

They lounged in bed for a while longer, engaged in some utterly shameless snuggling and enjoying each other's warmth, but then Dylan's stomach rumbled, and they were forced to consider the possibility of leaving their cocoon-of-ignoring-the-world. After a quick joint shower ending in traded handjobs, they dressed and headed downstairs to the kitchen, Dylan with his backpack in tow.

Christian and Max were already at the table, drinking coffee.

Upon spotting Rob and Dylan hand in hand, Max gave a disinterested nod. Christian's eyebrows shot up to his hairline, but he quickly smothered the expression.

"Mornin'," Dylan greeted, completely unfazed by any of the potential awkwardness in the situation.

"Morning," Christian replied, then checked his watch. "Well, afternoon, technically."

Max raised his mug to them. "Hey, Nugget. Dude screwing Nugget."

"Name's Dylan," Dylan said, still unperturbed. In fact, that may or may not have been a twitch of a smile at one corner of his mouth that Rob saw just then.

"Max. And this is Christian. We're Rob's roommates."

Dylan took a seat at the table like he belonged there and promptly unzipped his backpack, pulling out a stack of papers and a battered old netbook. "Hi. I'm his boyfriend."

Wow. Mister Let's-Not-Get-Too-Committed had apparently turned over a new leaf, because he was going all-out, what with dropping the "L" word this morning, and now introducing them as a couple? What was next, sitting next to Rob in class every day, forming their own two-man clique?

Before this point, Rob had been willing to believe the "starting to love you" speech had just been Dylan's orgasm talking, or maybe Dylan was more free with the word than other men, like maybe he said it to everyone he had good sex with. Or maybe he'd meant "love" the way you *love* cheesecake, or your computer's new graphics card, or that sexy-as-hell actor they'd cast to play opposite Katherine Heigl in her latest forgettable rom-com.

But now Rob wasn't so sure. Especially since he'd already established that Dylan was the kind of person who had to vocalize just about every thought that crossed his mind.

Was it really so hard to believe someone could love him? Or was it just because it was so damn soon?

Or was it the fact that Dylan didn't even know him at all?

Rob sighed, the lightness of his morning vanishing as new guilt and worries settled on his shoulders. "Coffee, Dylan? Tea? Something to eat? I have sugary kids' cereal, or I can make us some eggs and toast if you want."

"Is the sugary kids' cereal multicolored?" Dylan asked, still smiling at him with that dopey expression. Yeah, he was definitely sincere with the love thing.

"No, but it has marshmallows?" Rob couldn't help smiling back. He put the kettle on.

"Good enough. Okay. Gimme a bowl and don't skimp on the marshmallows. And a coffee, please. Black." He opened his laptop just as Rob returned to the cupboards, searching out the box of cereal. "Usually it's me making breakfast the next morning," Dylan told Max and Christian, obviously pleased with the change.

Rob poured two bowls of cereal and sloshed in milk. Unlike Max, he didn't have to sniff it before he did. "Well, you brought me dinner last night. Next time you can take me out for bacon and eggs."

"I'll do you one better. I'll make you Belgian waffles."

"You gonna bring a Belgian waffle maker along with you on a booty call?" Max asked. "Okay, Nugget, you can keep him."

"Good to know I have your permission," Rob said with a snort as he turned, setting both bowls of cereal on the table. Spoons next, and Dylan's coffee, and then the kettle was whistling, so he made himself a tea. "Not that I needed it in the first place."

"Hell, yes, you fuckin' need my permission," Max retorted. "You think I'm gonna just let any loser off the street bone my favorite little guy and break his heart?"

Christian sputtered, Rob bristled, but it was Dylan who was quickest with a comeback: "From where I'm sitting, you're not much bigger than he is, *little guy*."

Christian burst out in one of his rare laughs, or did until Max punched him in the shoulder for it, at least.

"This guy knows what I'm talking about," Dylan said, gesturing to Christian by poking his lips out.

Rob smiled to himself as he sat down with his tea, scraping his rickety chair across the floor until his and Dylan's thighs were touching under the table. He hunched over Dylan's computer and saw it was open to their project PowerPoint, where Dylan had dutifully started typing up Rob's notes. Seeing that Rob was looking, Dylan tabbed through the presentation to the slide on *My Marilyn*. "Noticed your notes were a little sketchy on this piece," he said with a mischievous smirk.

"Huh," Rob replied, taking a thoughtful sip of his hot tea. Felt great on his slightly battered throat. "*Something* must have distracted me."

"It was my sexual magnetism," Dylan clarified with a sage nod.

Max slapped his palms on the table. "*Well*, that's breakfast over. How about we find something to distract *us* for a few hours, babe?" He waggled his eyebrows at Christian meaningfully. Was he . . . was he trying to one-up Dylan?

"Nice meeting you, Dylan," Christian said, absolutely unflustered by any of it. But then, he'd had plenty of time to get used to Max's antics by now. One breakfast with Dylan couldn't be much more shocking to him than living with Max already was.

"You too, Christian. And Max." Dylan gave a friendly wave, and once they'd gone, knocked shoulders with Rob. "So those are your roommates, eh? What're the odds of having three gay-or-at-least-bi guys in one house, do you think?"

"Who knows. Just too bad I couldn't have used those odds to win the lottery instead."

"You did win the lottery. The gay roommate lottery."

Rob turned his attention to his cereal. "I don't consider it a win unless I'm getting laid out of it."

"You tellin' me neither of those guys even tried to poke you?" Dylan stirred his own spoon in his bowl until he'd gathered an acceptable marshmallow-to-cereal ratio.

"Nope. To be honest, I'm surprised they even believe I had sex with *you*. Before this morning, I'd kinda half convinced myself they thought I reproduced asexually."

"What we did this morning was absolutely *not* about reproduction, Puny. That was pure for-pleasure, animal *sex*." Dylan's hand snaked around Rob's back, dipping down into the ass of his jeans. "So it's their loss for not seeing what an insatiable little slut you are."

"Oh, quit it with the sweet talk, you're making me blush." Rob scoffed, then forced himself to return his attention back to their school work. "So is this stack of paper the stuff I missed?"

"Yeah. Notes, mostly, and then printouts of the first two group presentations. You missed a *very* stimulating analysis of woven tapestries."

"Wow, now I'm really sad you decided to give me a BJ in the rain."

Dylan flashed a toothy smile, brilliant but over quick. "Oh, and also, we got a handout for our final project. Doctor Chastity reserved the gallery space for a one-night show. We have to do self-portraits."

"Self-portraits, seriously?" Rob groaned. "Is this tenth-grade art? We going to have to do construction paper silhouette cutouts next?"

"Don't give her any ideas. So the assignment is to do a self-portrait that's *not* in our preferred medium, and then a write-up of three techniques or basic elements of art we chose to use. So if you make use of negative space, you have to explain how you did it and why you chose that."

"On a self-portrait. Ugh. And I can't even do a sculptural piece?"

"Yep. And I can't do comic art. Which is really too bad because I had a really great idea to do a riff on one of those forties-style jingoistic Captain America or Superman covers but with me as the villain."

Rob couldn't help grinning at that. It sounded pretty cool, actually. Totally Dylan's style. "How do you do a racist caricature of an Inuit?"

"Okay, okay, get this, right?" Dylan made an expansive gesture, setting the scene. "The Eskimo! The man with a heart of ice *walks among you*! I'd be wearing a very menacing parka."

"You should totally do it anyway," Rob said with a snorting giggle, stuck on the idea of a menacing parka. "It sounds amazing. So what are you going to do instead?"

"I'll probably just do some bullshit abstract piece of crap, make up a slick story to go with it. Or maybe I'll do the old polar-bear-in-a-snowstorm blank canvas thing, except I'm the bear, and then I'll play it totally serious like 'this is an image that's very sacred to my ancestors.' What about you? Any ideas yet?"

"No fucking clue."

CHAPTER 14

Whether he'd planned to or not, Rob was living a double life. At work, he was Bobby, cute and flirtatious, the darling of his customers. All it had taken to balance his two halves was to trade away the video store shifts that Dylan came in for like clockwork, and since that trade involved taking Max's Friday night shift, it had been a painless process. *Voilà*: he was free to keep his boyfriend, and still be Bobby some of the time, too.

And the rest of the time he was a slightly improved version of Rob, a Rob who had someone to sit with in class, a Rob who spent more time with his real-life roommates and sister than with his Kingdom of Elves guild. A Rob with an actual *boyfriend*, someone who spent time with him not out of obligation, but out of affection. Someone to fuck and joke around with and cuddle and bicker with.

Having a safety valve to let off those Bobby-urges seemed to help make his day-to-day life as Rob more palatable. Easier to navigate. Or maybe that was just the confidence he got out of being in a relationship with Dylan. They'd even made plans to go out to Celebrities with Bernice and her girlfriends. He'd had to pay Dylan to go along with *that* one with an extended rimming session, but since Rob didn't mind rimming and Dylan wanted to meet his sister—even if it meant going to Celebrities with a bunch of shrieking straight girls—neither of them was feeling the least bit cheated by their bargain.

Yes, being with Dylan hadn't "fixed" Rob's urge to be Bobby, but he'd successfully drawn a line between Bobby and Rob, neatly keeping the two halves of himself separate . . . except when they weren't.

Like right now. Dylan in Rob's bed, lying back, Rob straddling him, riding his huge dick like a very enthusiastic cowgirl. And for all his intentions to keep Bobby out of his relationship, there she was. Because yeah, Dylan might be fucking his ass, but Rob couldn't help picturing Dylan fucking his sloppy, wet pussy instead. Pounding it, filling every last inch of space, and God, yeah, looking up and watching with admiration as Bobby's tits bounced, as Bobby's pretty nipples tightened into perfect little peaks. He couldn't help it. He reached down to where Dylan's hands cupped his waist and guided them upward, up to cup his tits, hold them and weigh them as they jiggled and bobbed.

"Yes," Bobby moaned, losing himself to the wonderful fantasy, and Dylan's thumbs flicked his nipples, and Dylan's hands squeezed and kneaded his little tits.

"Gonna come for me, baby?" Dylan asked, circling Bobby's nipples with the pads of his thumbs as he pushed Bobby's tits together, creating a sexy little line of cleavage.

Pussy clenching that big, invading dick, tossing his head back with a wild, high cry, Bobby did.

"So beautiful," Dylan murmured into his hair when it was over, cradling Rob to his chest, just *holding* him as he trembled with shivers that he couldn't attribute solely to either pleasure or shame. "My beautiful baby, my beautiful baby."

That was when Rob knew he was lost.

No denying it anymore. Something had to give.

Friday night. Celebrities night. Rob had agreed to meet Dylan after work at a little sushi restaurant he liked. They could have dinner together and make a game plan before meeting up with Bernice and her friends at the bar.

Rob had packed his good jeans and a nice, black, button-down shirt to wear, but for now he was in his Bobby-wear, trying not to look at the clock too conspicuously as Charlie VIP droned on about how much more sexual freedom there was in Mexico.

Please don't mention the merits of bestiality. Please don't mention the merits of bestiality.

Luckily it never got to that point, although there was no denying that was the angle Charlie had been driving at the entire "conversation." Charlie was more on the clueless and socially stunted end of the creeper scale versus the aggressive one, which meant that after a few nonanswers, he eventually gave up on this particular horrible quest and wandered off on another one: combing the store in search of this week's depravity.

Thank God.

Once Charlie had gone again, leaving the store empty and Bobby with only a *slightly* grimy feeling all over his body as a result of their extended interactions, Bobby was able to resume watching the clock again in earnest. Just before nine. If it was slow in the hour leading up to closing, he could easily be out of here by ten after eleven and at the restaurant ten minutes after that. So a little more than two and a half hours until he got to see Dylan.

Or zero minutes zero seconds, even.

Because that was Dylan strolling right through the front door right now.

And looking straight at Bobby.

Well, Bobby *had* recently resolved that this whole double life thing he'd been doing wasn't tenable, hadn't he? Of course, he hadn't planned on coming out quite like this. It wasn't fair to either of them. He was about to open his mouth and say exactly that, but Dylan beat him to it. "Oh! Sorry, uh, I thought Rob was supposed to be working tonight."

You have got to be fucking kidding me.

But there was no smile, no gotcha moment, nothing. Dylan was seriously standing there, looking right fucking at him, and not recognizing who he was. And sure, that kind of thing had been far-fetched but possible when they'd first known each other, but they'd spent every single day together for weeks now. Far-fetched should be outright impossible by now, but there Dylan was, staring at him without even the tiniest glint of recognition in his eyes.

Well, fuck. What now?

The smart thing, of course, would be to say, "Dylan, it's me," in his Rob voice, force Dylan to see the two halves of himself coalesce into one.

But apparently Bobby wasn't feeling up to being smart just now, because when he spoke, it was with Bobby's voice, even more carefully feminine than usual. "Oh, um, yeah. You're his boyfriend, right? He wanted to go home early and get ready for tonight. He said that if you came in, to tell you he's still planning on meeting you at the restaurant."

Dylan's face fell, and he scrubbed the toe of his grody, old sneaker across the floor. "Oh. Okay."

Wow, for a cross-dresser, Bobby was kind of terrible at lying. *Well, duh. Because being Bobby isn't a fucking lie for you, remember? No more a lie than being Rob is.* "Sorry?" he tried.

"Don't be. It's fine."

The thing about Dylan was, he was a terrible fucking liar too. It wasn't fine. It wasn't fine at all.

Just tell him it's you. Just tell him. Tell him it's you and you love him and you're sorry but this is who you really are.

But he couldn't.

He just . . . couldn't. What if Dylan was grossed out? Insulted him? What if Dylan dumped him? What if . . . what if Dylan *hurt* him?

No. Dylan wouldn't hurt him. Not physically, anyway. He was a good guy, Bobby knew.

But being good didn't preclude him from any of those other reactions, and Bobby wasn't ready to let this go. Wasn't ready to face the consequences, whatever they were.

And it didn't really matter now anyway, because Dylan was already walking right out the door without another word.

Hands trembling, lip wobbling, Bobby reached up with careful dignity to take off his glasses. Folded the arms closed and set them down on the counter just so. Didn't get a chance to cry like he'd planned to, because the bell over the door jingled again.

Dylan?

Nope, that ship had sailed. It was Adam Hollister Cap, who gave him a grin. "Like you without the glasses, babycakes."

Bobby blushed and sniffled. "Um, thanks."

"No prob. You okay? You look like somebody just slapped you."

"Something like that. But never mind. I'm fine now." To prove it, he smiled, and reached for his glasses again, as proof of his inward resolution not to cry.

"Do you need those to see?" Adam asked.

Bobby shook his head.

"You should leave them off, then. For me." Adam smiled, eyebrows up. The expression was a little lecherous, but flattering nonetheless.

That was right. Bobby was attractive and sweet, and if Dylan didn't see that, then he didn't need Dylan.

Just wanted him. So bad.

He'd come out. He would. Tonight at dinner, he'd tell Dylan everything, and if Dylan didn't like it, or shamed him for it, well, then he'd start over. Find someone new.

Not Adam and his creepy fetish videos, though. Bobby had *some* standards, thank you.

When he looked at Adam again, it was with renewed confidence. "Can I help you with something?" he asked, no cracks in his voice.

"Yeah. I was wondering if you could . . . advise me on something."

"Sure!" Bobby said, and stood.

Adam led him to the wall of toys. "I was thinking of getting one of these cock ring things. I heard some of them can help girls come when you're fucking them."

"Oh, yes," Bobby agreed. "The vibrating ones, definitely, and some of them have attachments meant to hit her clit while you fuck her."

"Uh-huh?" Adam asked, eyelids dropping low at that last part. "And which would *you* . . . suggest?"

Yikes. Better pull this back to professionalism again. "Well, this one's a pretty good seller." Bobby stepped forward, taking off the wall a bright blue silicone ring with a leaping dolphin attached. "The dolphin has a vibrator in it. Basically turns your junk into one of those rabbits girls love so much."

Wrong move, he realized, when that step forward put him between the wall and Adam, who suddenly lunged forward.

"Um," he protested when Adam boxed him in, one arm pressed to the wall on either side of him.

"Don't act like you're surprised," Adam said. "Look me in the eye and tell me you don't want to try that gadget out with me right now in that little booth over there." He nodded toward the disgusting peep show booths with a leer.

Bobby dropped the sex toy package like it had burned his palm. Looked Adam in the eye, as requested, but this close, he couldn't help but notice the size difference between them as if for the first time.

How much he had to tilt his face up just to look Adam in the eyes. But he stood his ground. "I don't. Sorry."

"Tease. Sounds like you need a little convincing."

Bobby was about to ask how *convincing* it would be if he put his knee in Adam's balls, but that was when Adam moved again, this time grabbing Bobby's shoulder in one hand and cupping Bobby's crotch in the other.

Adam's eyes bugged out for a second, and then his expression turned cruel. The hand between Rob's legs flew up to grab his shoulder instead, keeping him roughly pinned. "What the fuck?"

"Let me go," Rob warned, dropping the girl voice. "Let me go *right now*, or I'll call the cops."

Swing and a miss. "Oh yeah? And what's your little lying tranny self gonna tell 'em?"

"My little lying tranny self is gonna tell them you sexually assaulted me, that's what."

Adam gave Rob a hard shake, bashing the back of his head into the wall. The sharp pain in the back of his head turned to rolling nausea in his stomach. "Yeah? Well, in that case, I'll tell them *you* came on to *me*. Maybe even wanted me to pay you. Sucky sucky five dolla. You versus me. Who you think they're gonna believe?"

"You willing to take that risk?" Rob bit out. It took all the bravery he had, all the bravery he *should* have had with Dylan ten minutes ago. Maybe if he'd been honest, Dylan would be here right now. Dylan would be here, talking it out with him, maybe angry, maybe confused, maybe even grossed out, but he'd be *here*, and Rob would be safe. Or maybe he wouldn't be here at all.

Adam smiled, baring teeth. "Are *you*?"

God, what if they *didn't* believe him? Yeah, there was camera footage of what had just gone on between them, but cops fucked up cases like this all the time, even with all the evidence in the world to at their disposal. And he had to face the facts: Rob was a cross-dressing Asian kid working in a seedy porn store. And what if Adam was a Good Kid, a sports star, the son of someone important or well connected, a beloved meathead in the community? A whole new nausea overtook Rob's body. "My boyfriend," he yelped as a final gamble. "He's coming to pick me up. Look, just let me go. Nothing has to come of this. I won't call the cops, okay? I won't even tell my boyfriend about what happened. Just let me go."

That threat—plea?—seemed to stick better than the one about the cops, because Adam released Rob and backed off just enough that Rob was able to squeeze by him and make a sprint for the counter. Panic button safely in reach again, he took a deep, shaky breath.

Across the store by the toy wall, Adam calmly stooped to pick up the dolphin cock ring and return it to its proper place on the wall. Then, like nothing had happened between them at all, he headed for the DVD racks, browsed awhile, and finally returned to the counter with his selection. Fucking sociopath.

Rob checked him out, trying not to let the shaking in his hands show. But if he really wanted to prove he wasn't afraid, he'd have to make eye contact. He forced himself to look Adam in the face, and it filled him with cold dread to see no defeat there. *You're not getting rid of me that easy*, Adam's expression said. *You outsmarted me this time, but I'll be back.*

Someone braver and smarter with more resources and support might have looked right back at him with eyes full of *And I'll be ready*. But Rob didn't have any of those things. Without Bobby and Dylan, he had nothing. He *was* nothing.

Why had he ever tried to convince himself otherwise?

CHAPTER 15

T he hour before closing that night *was* slow, and Rob *was* out of the store by ten after eleven. But when he'd set the alarm and locked the door behind him, he didn't go to the restaurant to meet Dylan, or to Celebrities to meet his sister and her friends.

He went home. Alone.

It wasn't even the fact that Adam had put hands on him that had done Rob in and broken him down. Sure, his shoulders and the back of his head kind of hurt, but that pain would subside. He definitely had reason to be afraid of Adam, but not because he posed a physical threat. After all, if he'd wanted to hurt Rob, he could have.

Which, strangely enough, was a horrifying and shocking realization all on its own: even if Adam specifically posed no threat, dressing up as Bobby was fucking *dangerous*. All it took was one hateful person, one moment alone, one . . .

God, he didn't even want to think about it.

It wasn't the physical hurt that sent him home alone now. It wasn't the fear of how much worse that hurt could get, the cold reality of the danger that he'd been ignoring all these weeks while he was high on the exhilaration of being flirted with and paid attention to. Wasn't even the disgust in Adam's voice or the things he'd said or the hurtful slurs he'd used to say them.

Part of it was guilt and shame. What-ifs, swirling in his head on the bus ride home like toxic fumes. What if he had been honest with Dylan? What if he hadn't responded positively to Adam's flirting and compliments? What if he hadn't left the protection of the counter? What if he hadn't used such sexual language describing the toy? What if he'd kneed Adam in the junk? Called Adam's bluff on not being afraid of the cops? Not acted so damn afraid and pitiful, leaving Adam with the upper hand, ensuring that he'd be back?

So many things gone wrong. So many opportunities wasted. So many bad, cowardly choices. But he could talk himself out of all that, eventually, mostly. It wasn't like Rob was any stranger to racism and harassment and confrontations gone wrong. When the pain was fresh he beat himself up about it, but eventually he could look at things logically, forgive himself, move forward. All necessary skills, because otherwise the guilt would kill him.

What he *couldn't* move forward from was the fact that all his precious illusions about Bobby had been shattered.

Bobby didn't make him braver, or smarter, or more outgoing, or any of it. On the inside, he'd always just be Rob.

And despite all the jealousy he felt for his sister, being a woman didn't magic away problems, either. It created new ones. Irritating new ones, like Charlie and his gross flirtation, but harmful ones too. Because Adam hadn't lured or assaulted him knowing he was some cross-dressing freak. He'd done all those things thinking Bobby was a woman. An attractive, outgoing, *real* woman.

It had been a play act, all of it. He'd wanted the perks of being a woman without the downfalls. Wanted to play dress-up without committing to any biological or lifestyle changes. All that time he'd been talking himself into believing it wasn't a lie, that Bobby was a genuine part of his identity, it'd been bullshit. He had a kink, and he had an inferiority complex when it came to his sister, and he had a stupid, rosy vision of what being a woman was, and all of that had combined into a dumb fucking scheme, and now it was biting him in the ass.

His phone buzzed for what felt like the hundredth time and he finally took it out of his bag, half tempted to throw the fucking thing out the bus window.

Missed call: Dylan
Missed call: Dylan
Text from Dylan
Text from Dylan
Text from Dylan
Text from Bernice
Text from Bernice
Missed call: Dylan

Missed call: Bernice

He settled for turning it off instead.

An hour or so later, he dragged himself up the front steps of the house and into the living room where Max was playing video games with Austin. "Hey, um, Max?" Rob said.

Max normally wouldn't stand for being interrupted in the middle of a shoot-'em-up, but he must have heard something in Rob's tone, because he paused the game, blatantly ignoring Austin when he bitched him out for it. He turned to Rob. "Yeah?"

"You know how . . ." Rob twisted his mouth, almost chewing his words. "You know what you said about . . . about not letting just any guy . . . Well, anyway, I was wondering if you could put your money where your mouth was on the whole protecting-me thing."

Now a genuine look of concern came over Max's features. "What is it, Nugget? What happened? Are you okay? Jesus, you're shaking." He moved to get up off the couch, but Rob stopped him with a raised hand.

Rob *was* shaking, though. He grabbed two fistfuls of his jeans to try to steady his hands. "I'm fine. I just . . . If Dylan comes by, I need you to not let him in to see me, okay? He didn't hurt me, but I don't want to see him right now."

Couldn't face Dylan after everything had happened, not when Rob'd stood him up like the pathetic coward he was, and especially not when maybe being honest with Dylan about who he was, when he'd had the chance, could have prevented this whole fucking mess. If he saw Dylan now, would he correct that error—too little, too late—or would he keep his secret and learn nothing at all from his past mistake? It was a lose-lose situation, and Rob was tired of playing the game.

Even Austin was looking at Rob with an expression of pity now.

"Sure," Max said gently. "Of course. You're sure you're okay?"

"Just shaken up," Rob replied. "Promise. Going to bed now."

An hour or so later, Rob heard the yelling coming from downstairs. Max's raised voice. Dylan's much softer one. And then the door slammed and Dylan was gone and Rob rolled over, pulled the blankets over his head, and went to sleep.

CHAPTER 16

C reating a self-portrait when you didn't even know who or what you were, now that was a fucking joke.

Rob tore the page from his sketchbook, balled it up, and tossed it into the trash with the others. Even if he *had* been allowed to work in his own medium, he still wouldn't have been able to come up with a concept for this piece. He was so confused. So fragmented. So drowned in self-pity and self-hatred.

But then, why bother at all? It wasn't like he was planning on going to school come Monday anyway. He'd already emailed Doctor Chastity to tell her that he'd come down with another crippling illness. Luckily, she wasn't enough of a hardass to ask for a doctor's note, but then, if she had, he'd have just dropped the class entirely. Taken the ugly Withdrawal on his GPA and redone the class once Dylan wasn't in it.

Pathetic.

He couldn't summon up the balls to just come out to Dylan already, but he couldn't break up with the guy, either. Didn't have it in him to lie about the reason. Hell, didn't even want to face the questions why. He was a class-A coward.

After all, hadn't the Bobby thing just proved that Rob was a master at avoiding rather than confronting his issues?

Problems with making friends and influencing people? Don't bother changing your behavior, just make up a female persona to do it all for you!

Don't want your boyfriend to dump you, but don't want to dump him, either? Just drop out of school and never speak to him again!

Hell, right back to that night with Mike. Afraid of saying no to a guy when he's about to ask a potentially awkward question? Just stop speaking to him, even if it means losing a good friend and flaking on your guild responsibilities!

Oh yeah, Rob had an idea for a self-portrait all right. He flipped to a new page of his sketchbook, grabbed a thick black marker, and wrote the word *LOSER* in all capital letters, the word so big it took up every inch of space on the page. That about covered it.

He closed his sketchbook in disgust and logged on to his new Kingdom of Elves account. A buff human warrior in head to toe armor that actually covered his vital organs. Collect twenty-seven wolf spleens. Okay. He sure as hell had nothing better to do.

Rob didn't go to school the following Monday. Or Tuesday, for that matter. Didn't work on his assignments, including the self-portrait whose deadline was fast approaching. Didn't leave his room much at all, except to piss or to eat, the latter of which he only did at times he could be reasonably sure he wouldn't have run-ins with his roommates. Didn't answer his phone when it rang; Dylan had stopped calling after that first night, but Bernice persisted with her usual tenacity. Didn't do much of anything but grind, leveling his new human warrior from one to sixty in record time.

Wednesday, however, was a different story. Not on the school side of things, no, because Rob still skipped the day's classes, but there was no skipping his shift at Rear Entrance Video. After all, if he flunked any of his classes, he had a feeling that the money he was getting from his parents would dry up. In that case, a job would definitely come in handy.

From now on, though, Rob would earn the paychecks, not Bobby. Sure, he still had the whole getup in his bag, but he wouldn't put it on. Not tonight, not ever again. Time to leave Bobby, and all the trouble she represented, behind. Maybe after going cold turkey for a while, he could finally throw out the Bobby bag once and for all and just do what normal cross-dressers did. Gather a collection of bras and pantyhose and wear them for sexual kicks in the privacy of his own bedroom. Not like he had a boyfriend or friends anymore who could accidentally stumble upon them.

When he got to the store, he dropkicked his bag under the counter and took a seat next to Austin, who was working the dayshift. Thank God. He couldn't stand the thought of bearing Noah's or Max's or Christian's concern right now.

Austin wouldn't ask any questions. He was too busy avoiding eye contact and awkwardly clearing his throat to make any expressions of pity.

They worked side by side in (relative) silence as they counted out the till, and Rob was just thinking how maybe he could do this, maybe he could go back to being a normal lonely guy, and then the bell over the door chimed.

Adam, of course. Because who else could it *possibly* be? Rob never thought he'd see the day when he wished Charlie VIP would come around more often.

"Hey, man," Austin greeted.

Rob stared hard at the bills in his hands, like counting by fives had suddenly become the most difficult calculation he'd ever attempted.

"Hey." Adam's voice was close. Definitely standing right over him. Rob tossed his head a little, hoping his bangs would fall over his eyes. Maybe Adam wouldn't recognize him. Ha, fat chance. Who did Rob think the guy was, Dylan? "Where's that little Asian cutie you guys got working nights?" Adam was a shit actor; there was no denying he knew full well that the "little Asian cutie" was sitting right under his nose.

"Little Asian cutie? I don't—oh, do you mean *Rob*?"

Shit, Rob had to look up now. He lifted his chin, staring at Adam like he didn't recognize him. Adam, unperturbed, just smirked back. "Nah. This was definitely a girl."

Austin shook his head, totally oblivious to the tension between Adam and Rob. Too busy being thankful that whatever it was, it wasn't gay. "No chicks work here, man. Not for a long time."

Bad actor Adam now plastered a look of fake shock on his face. "Really? I could have sworn there was one here when I came in the other night. Actually, she looked a lot like—"

"Must have been a different store," Rob snapped. *Fine. Whatever you want from me, whatever you're playing at, fine. You win. Just don't ruin my life any more than you—no, I—already have.*

"Must have," Adam said, playing it off without comment. "Oh, well. Gonna go pick out a DVD now." With one last sneer, he made for the DVD racks.

Austin closed the till and turned to Rob like everything was totally normal. "Well, that's it for me. You okay here?"

No! Please don't leave, please!

But if he asked, then he'd have to reveal why. Not to mention that whatever Adam wanted, he'd be willing to wait for it. If not today, then another day. All Rob was doing was delaying the inevitable. There was no avoiding whatever unstated pact he and Adam had just made. He felt sick to his stomach. And at the same time, he felt . . . calm. *Yes. This is what I asked for. This is what I deserve.* "Yeah, have a good night, okay?"

"You too," Austin said, and since he couldn't get away from Rob fast enough, he fled.

Alone with Adam again. All Rob had to do was wait for him to reveal himself. What he wanted. What price Rob would have to pay.

And there he was, emerging from behind a rack of DVDs and heading straight for the counter.

"I liked you better with long hair," he said.

"Clip-in extensions. And that's funny, because I liked you when you were just a garden variety racist dickbag without the blackmail material." Rob glared at him, suddenly refusing to act submissive to this man. He'd give Adam what he wanted, pay whatever it cost to keep this secret, but that didn't mean Rob had to make it *enjoyable* for the creep. Maybe if he wasn't crying and protesting, Adam wouldn't be able to get it up. "Actually, scratch that. I never liked you. So c'mon, out with it. What do you want?"

Victory. For one second, Adam was thrown off guard, but it passed quickly. "Clip-in extensions, was it? You got them with you?"

He was too pissed off to lie. "Yep. And the makeup and the tits. Is that what you want, then?" *Fucker.* "For me to get all dressed up for you?" So this was what it felt like to have nothing left to lose. He wondered if that was where Dylan got some of his trademark fuck-the-world bravado from. "So if I'm the tranny pervert here, what does that make you, exactly?"

Adam's lip curled. "You should be flattered I want you at all. Most guys like me would just kick the ass of little ladyboys like you."

If that was supposed to be scary, it didn't work. Faced with the alternatives—being outed, being raped—getting the shit kicked out of him didn't seem that bad. Hey, maybe he could even get a couple of punches in, himself.

But no way was Adam going to give Rob the option of fighting back, whatever he did. He was a petty tyrant. A coward. Too bad Rob was an even bigger one, because otherwise it would have been easy to strip Adam of his dubious power.

"So, anyway, here's how it's going to go. You're going to lock the front door of the store. Then you're going to go into that gross little cum booth and put on the hair and the makeup and the tits and the whole nine yards while I watch." Rob listened carefully, trying not to let any of his fear or disgust show on his face. Becoming Bobby had always been a private ritual, a sweet, empowering transformation, and now it was . . . twisted. Well, at least maybe this would fix him. If he had negative associations with dressing up, then maybe he wouldn't *crave* it so bad anymore. "And you're going to wear these."

Adam took a plastic bag out of the pocket of his hoodie and dumped out its contents on the counter. Red lace. Rob should have known. He swallowed a gag. "Fine." With shaking hands, he took the cheap lace underwear. Bent under the front counter to pick up his bag with makeup and hair and the rest of it. The panic button was right there, right within reach. All he had to do was—

"Door," Adam instructed, startling Rob upright again.

Window of opportunity closed.

"Yeah, yeah." *Fucker.* As rebellious as he was feeling inside, though, with the panic button out of reach again Rob's choices were down to doing as he was told, or accepting whatever combination of getting beaten up and outed that Adam decided to inflict on him. So he dutifully locked the door under Adam's watchful gaze, then headed straight for the peepshow booth. *Doing what you want. Everything you want. Your little pet freak putting on a fashion show.* "There's no mirror," he said, stalling, afraid to cross that last threshold.

"Don't need one, because you're gonna be looking at me the whole time."

Correction: sick fucker.

Well, if Adam wanted to get off on watching Rob suffer, on humiliating him, then he wasn't going to get it. Rob wasn't going to play the crying victim, not for this sicko. What was it Dylan had said? *Prisoner of war.* Defeated, pinned by perverse voyeuristic gazes, but still with his dignity. He'd turn his brain off. Let his body run on autopilot. Minimize pain.

So you're still a coward, but now you're a clever one. Whatever lets you sleep at night.

Yeah, actually. That. Rob would have rather done anything but get into that small, dark space, beyond the reach of the store's cameras, but it was what Adam wanted, and at the moment what Adam wanted, Adam got. All Rob had to do was not make any trouble, and it would all be over soon. Like a man going to his execution, he stepped into the booth and turned to face Adam, who now blocked the entrance and had pulled the curtain shut behind him.

Let's get this over with.

Adam loomed over him, watching in grim silence as Rob stripped down. He kept his movements economical. Didn't let himself linger or hesitate. Looked Adam right in the eyes as he tucked himself and pulled on the panties Adam had chosen. Didn't even curl in on himself when Adam's hungry gaze roamed down Rob's body, down to the tacky underwear he'd oh-so-carefully selected, covering the flatness where Rob's cock and balls should be.

No shame. No shame. No shame.

He's the one who should be ashamed. For making me do this. For his terrible fucking taste in underwear.

Because dammit, Rob sure as hell had nothing to be ashamed of. Well, he was ashamed of the cowardice, maybe—okay, definitely—but Bobby? Being Bobby was okay, even after being stripped of glamour and mystique until all that was left were chicken fillet bra inserts and surgical tape.

The transformation into Bobby felt fucking *good*. Dylan couldn't take that from him—not that he'd ever shown signs of being the sort of person who'd want to, if he knew—and if Dylan couldn't, then neither could Adam. No matter what Adam did. Made Rob do. No matter how much it hurt. No matter how much of a coward it made Rob to play along.

So sure, maybe this act tainted Rob, but *Bobby* was untouchable. In fact, this wasn't even her. Just Rob, standing here, skinny and covered in goose bumps, wearing nothing but hideous women's panties. Because Bobby wouldn't be fucking caught dead in something so incredibly tacky.

And after all his unspoken threats and aggressive need, Adam wasn't even touching Rob. Wasn't kissing him. Wasn't shoving him face-first into the wall. Nothing. He was just . . . standing there. Trapping him, but simultaneously somehow trapped himself.

The worst of the fear settled to a muted numbness, and Rob dressed as quickly as he'd undressed, covering up the hideous "sexy" underwear and feeling instantly better for it. The extensions came next, not so difficult to do without a mirror, he didn't think. The makeup. He'd never put on mascara while glaring at someone before, but it felt kinda good. His hands weren't even shaking, even though his heart was pounding like he'd run a marathon.

"So pretty," Adam said at last, the first time he'd spoken since closing them both up in the booth. It was like he'd been in a trance. Still was, by the way his fingers caught Rob's hair and brushed it back behind his shoulder, like they were lovers. "You—"

"Rob? You in here?"

Dylan. Rob had never been so relieved and terrified in his whole life.

"What the fuck?" Adam snarled, that gentle hand in Rob's hair instantly turning into a tight, punishing fist. "How did he get in here? I watched you lock the door!"

"Why the hell do you think it's called Rear Entrance Video, you dumb shit?" Rob's voice came out deep and furious and masculine. The spell between them broke. "Now let me . . . go!" He hauled back, pushed Adam hard with both hands and every ounce of body weight he had. Rob's clip-in tore with a horrible ripping pain along his scalp, and then Adam fell through the curtain.

"Holy shit!" Dylan shouted as Rob came tumbling out after him.

Adam, on his ass on the floor, got one look at Dylan: six feet tall, two hundred pounds plus and broad-shouldered, looking like a punk in his ERASE RACISM sweatshirt, and *bolted.* The front door jingled open and slammed closed again.

"What the . . ." Dylan watched Adam go, then turned back to Rob, who was standing in front of the peep show booth, hands still balled into fists, heart pounding and trembling—oh, so *there* was the adrenaline. "What the hell is going on here? Who is that guy?" And then, a little hesitantly, "Are you okay, Bobby?"

"Oh for fuck's sake, Dylan!" Rob shouted without thinking. Well, trying to keep Rob and Bobby separate had caused this whole mess in the first place. "It's me, Rob, you goddamn idiot. You know, your—" *Can't really call myself his anything, now, anything but . . .* "—ex."

"I—"

"Just fucking look at me, damn you! Look at me! Are you fucking blind?" Tears started to streak down Rob's cheeks, and before he could stop himself, he was tearing his extensions out, clip by clip, yanking them hard enough his real hair tore. He didn't care. Who fucking cared about hair, real or fake, girl or boy. The mangled black locks fell to the floor. "Yes! *I'm* Bobby! Your fucked-up boyfriend is—"

Dylan grabbed him by the shoulders, pinning his arms down to keep him from hurting himself any more. "I know. Do you fucking hear me? I know!"

What?

"I always knew, you fucking . . . you." Dylan sighed, letting Rob go so he could rub his temples. "I was just waiting for you to tell me. For you to *trust* me enough. But you never fucking did, did you? And what was I supposed to do? I didn't want to embarrass you."

"You . . ."

"And I kept trying to hint that I knew, and I kept trying to give you chances to be honest with me, but you never fucking took them. Did you think I was gonna hurt you? Did you think I wouldn't keep your secret? Did you think I was gonna judge you or try to change you or something?"

Rob's chest burned. He was feeling light-headed. "I don't know. I don't know what I was expecting. I just—I wanted to tell you, but I couldn't."

"You wanted to, but you couldn't?" Dylan snarled, raising his voice and making Rob flinch back despite himself. The terror, new and hideous, came rushing back. "You *couldn't*? So what, you just strung me along, and I'm supposed to be fine with that?"

"*Strung you along?*" Rob shouted back.

"Yeah, strung me along. Remember when we first met and I said I was gay? *Gay.* As in, I *only like men.* As in, if you knew this was where things were headed for you, then you should have fucking *told me.* Or hell, you didn't have to tell me, but you could have at least not gotten into a relationship with me."

"Where things were headed? And where are they headed, exactly?" *Tell me, oh wise one, because I have no fucking clue what's up with me. What's wrong with me.*

Dylan's face fell, his expression closing off. When he spoke again, it was in a monotone. "I don't know. You tell me."

"Shit." Rob wiped at one wet eye with the heel of his palm. He couldn't speak. Couldn't have answered the question Dylan was asking him even if he *could* speak.

"I'm sorry, Rob—Bobby—whatever you want to be called. I'm sorry for barging in here when I knew you didn't want to see me, and I'm sorry for yelling. But you need to sort your shit out. You can't just avoid me forever." He ran both hands through his hair, making it stand on end. "Or, well, you can avoid *me* I guess, but you can't avoid making a fucking decision about who you are and what you want."

"I don't know. I just don't know." Rob's legs were suddenly so weak he couldn't stand. He lowered himself to his knees on the floor and ducked his head, too ashamed to look Dylan in the eye.

Dylan blew out a harsh sigh. "Well, do me and everyone else in this world a favor, okay? Until you *do* know, don't use other people who fucking love you as lab rats for your gender experiments."

People who love you, Rob thought, dazed, as Dylan walked out on him.

CHAPTER 17

He wished he'd begged Dylan to stay with him until his shift was over, if not to talk it out then at least to keep him safe, but he'd been in shock and hurt and confused and he'd let Dylan walk right out the door.

And now that he was gone, there was no holding back the fear. The trembling. The nausea. He'd been granted a reprieve from whatever Adam had intended to do to him, and that brought the reality of the situation into sharp focus. He could have been raped. Filmed or photographed. Beaten up. Killed. Who knew what else.

Shivering so hard his teeth were chattering, he made it to the front of the store, where he promptly puked in the garbage can under the counter.

Lock the doors.

He stumbled in that direction. The front door, unlocked after Adam had used it to make his escape. The back door to the alley. He took a deep breath and returned to the safety of the counter. The chair seemed too dubious, dangerous somehow, so he sat on the floor. Not quite under the counter, but damn close to it.

Okay, safe for now. Nobody could get in. He couldn't get *out*, but nobody could get in. Good enough for now. Tourniquet tied.

God, was he going to stay in here all night until whoever was working days tomorrow showed up for their shift? No, because he was going to call Christian and tell him what had happened. Beg him not to ask questions, not to make Rob explain the whys or the hows.

Operating a smartphone when your hands were actually *vibrating* was a lot more difficult than he ever could have imagined, but he got it working. Christian answered on the third ring.

"Mmm, hello?" Fuck, he'd been asleep. Well, of course he had. The guy had more schoolwork than anyone Rob had seen, other than Bernice.

"Christian. Hey. Um, sorry for waking you up. It's Rob, by the way."

A tinge of concern crept into Christian's voice. "Is everything okay at the store?"

Rob took a deep breath. "No, Christian. No, it's not. And I need you to—" His voice broke. He sobbed. "I need you to not ask why, okay? But I need you to come down."

"Did we get robbed? Are you okay? Okay, don't hang up. I'm coming right now. Hang tight, buddy." Rob didn't hang up. Just put his phone down on the counter and tried to take a couple of deep breaths. Man, where was a paper bag when you needed one? Nowhere, that was where. Not like Dylan, who'd arrived at the most serendipitous time imaginable.

Wow. Dylan had saved him. He'd been humiliated and messed up and they'd fought, but Dylan had *saved* him. Jesus. Wow.

More deep breaths. He pictured himself in yoga class with Bernice. *Ujjayi breath*, the instructor reminded him in his head.

He didn't know how long he sat there on the floor, but out of nowhere there was a knock at the front door. He startled, got his breathing all messed up, heart working overtime again. Picked up his phone. Christian had never hung up on him. The call time read forty minutes. If he didn't have unlimited minutes, Rob was definitely going to have to pay him back. "Is that you?" he asked.

"It's us. Me and Max and Auntie Beverly. Come unlock the door, okay?"

That sick feeling returned. As if this wasn't humiliating enough, now he had a whole rescue party coming to his aid. He went to the door anyway. Unlocked it.

Auntie Beverly was the first one in, and she grabbed him by the shoulders and pulled him into a hug immediately. He barely fucking knew her, and by all rights touch should be the last thing he wanted right now, but he couldn't help but sink into her embrace. She was frail, but warm and solid at the same time, a mother with no children, a living contradiction, and he wouldn't trade her for the world. No wonder Christian loved her so much. She didn't speak. Didn't ask a single question.

Max did, though. "Rob? What are you wearing? Is that . . . is that mascara on your face?"

Shit, he'd been so fucking traumatized that he hadn't thought to get changed or take his makeup off. He was a total fuck-up.

"Never you mind," Auntie Beverly snapped at him, then pushed Rob out to arm's length and gave him a scrutinizing look. "Are you hurt, Rob?"

"No, ma'am," Rob said. "And no, the store didn't get robbed. Everything's fine here. I'm fine. I just need to go home now, okay? I need someone to take me home."

"Of course," Auntie Beverly said, nodding. "Of course you can go. Max, you and Rob take a cab back home and you get him showered and to bed. Christian, you can stay here with me and help close up."

"Got it," Christian said, taking his aunt's lead on the not-asking-questions thing.

"Rob, I'll find someone to cover your shifts for the next little bit. You just tell Christian when you're ready to work again, okay? And if it's never, that's okay too. Now go. Rest."

A coat fell around Rob's shoulders. Max. Max was helping dress him. Max had his backpack over one shoulder. And now Max had an arm around him. "C'mon, Nugget, you heard the boss lady. Let's go home and get you cleaned up."

Yes. Clean. That sounded like the best thing.

They didn't speak on the cab ride home. Max didn't let go of him. Touched Rob's shoulder, his elbow, his hand, let Rob lean against him as the cab made its seamless, dreamy way through Vancouver's streets. When they got home, Max helped him inside, turned on the water in the shower for him—near scalding, just the way he liked it—and left him. Once he'd undressed, Rob threw the red panties right in the trash and buried them under half a roll of wasted toilet paper.

He didn't know how long he stood in the shower's spray after that, standing and not cleaning himself, just letting the water run down him as it would. Long enough that the water ran cold, but in this house that could have been an hour or three minutes. Eventually, he got out. Didn't look at himself in the mirror, even just to check if the mascara running down his cheeks had been washed away. He could face himself tomorrow. Tonight he just wanted to sleep.

Except sleep didn't come. His mind circled restlessly, pacing through his newly horrifying memories. Adam. Dylan. Back and forth, back and forth, analyzing every detail. The things Dylan had said.

Don't use other people who fucking love you as lab rats for your gender experiments.

He had a lot to apologize for. A lot of people to apologize *to*.

Dylan. His sister. His roommates. Mike.

He'd fucked this up from the very start.

Well, since he wasn't fucking sleeping anyway . . .

He sat up in bed, smoothed his hair back with his millionth deep breath of the night, and headed for his computer.

Logged onto his abandoned Kingdom of Elves account. Unblocked Mike. Luckily, it was 2 a.m. on a weeknight, so Mike was online. Not messaging him, but online. Well, Rob had come this far.

FakeGeekGirl93: Hey Mike.

It took a few minutes, but at last a reply appeared.

LetsDoScience: Hello, stranger.

FakeGeekGirl93: I think I owe you an apology. Can we talk? On cam???

The video invitation popped up immediately.

No makeup, no extensions, no headband, no glasses, none of it. Rob accepted.

"Hi," he said.

Mike, with his massive headphones and wearing a T-shirt from a webcomic, put down his massive bottle of Mountain Dew and frowned. "Uh . . . hey."

"So, um, I guess by now you've figured out I'm, well . . ."

Mike's eyebrows shot up, and for a second it looked like he was about to laugh. "Username FakeGeekGirl. Fake geek girl. Ha-ha, I get it."

"Yeah. Fake girl, not fake geek. That's me." Rob waved timidly.

"So what, is this the part where you admit your plan all along was to lure me to some remote cabin in the woods?"

"I deserve that," Rob replied with a wince.

Mike didn't look angry, though. He looked sad. "No, you don't. Can I be honest with you? I kinda . . . knew."

No way!

Rob hadn't said it aloud, but Mike must have seen it on his face, because he nodded. "Yeah. From the time we, uh . . . had phone sex, actually. I mean, you have a good girl voice, but not *that* good."

"Oh." Rob's eyebrows stitched together. "So why did you ask me to take my shirt off then?"

"I never!" As generic and defensive as the protest was, Rob could see it all over Mike's face: he really hadn't. What was it with Rob? A consummate faker surrounded by honest men. "Oh shit, is that what you thought I was going to ask you? When you hung up on me all suddenly and blocked me?"

Rob blushed fiercely. "Um, yes?"

"Wow. Don't have a high opinion of me, huh? Well, for your information, I was going to ask for your address so I could send you a gift."

"A gift?"

"Yeah. Flowers. I know it's lame, but that's what girls do to me. They turn me lame."

"That's not lame, Mike. It's sweet!" Rob replied, unable to help the little bit of Bobby that seeped into the words. "But wait, by then you knew I was a guy. Why flowers?"

"I still *liked* you. I still do. Like you. I figured you were transgendered—"

"Transgender," Rob corrected gently.

Mike squirmed in his computer chair, eyes squinting at some middle distance. "Yeah. Sorry. Not up on the correct terminology. You know, born in a dude body but really a girl inside. Are you? Is that okay to ask? I should have read up on this stuff more. I got a pamphlet at the LGBT center on campus, but I never read it."

"I . . ." God, nobody had asked Rob that question directly before. He wasn't even sure how to answer it. "I don't think so? Actually, no. No, I'm not. I mean, I like my dick. I like being a guy. I just like being a girl sometimes too. And not just as a sex thing, which I think is an important distinction? Or feels like it should be? I guess I'm both. Guy and girl. But more guy."

Mike's face fell. "Oh. Because, you know, if you were a transgender, I mean, a transgender *girl*, that would be okay. I don't have like a fetish or anything, but I wouldn't mind." A pause, and then he added, "But since you're not, that doesn't mean we can't still be friends and everything. *Just* friends."

God, this guy was seriously too good to be true. Too bad Rob *wasn't* a girl.

Something clicked. Mike didn't care that he cross-dressed. Didn't judge him for it, didn't think less of him, didn't care about his genitals or his chromosomes. All he wanted was to date a girl.

How Rob saw *himself*, that was what mattered.

All Dylan wanted was to date a guy.

Rob was a guy. A guy who didn't always look or sound or dress like a guy, but definitely not a girl, either.

That was why Dylan had wanted an answer. That was why he'd been afraid to commit. He'd known about Rob's cross-dressing from the start, but he hadn't known what it *meant*. Hadn't known if Rob was considering making the change to Bobby permanently.

Who I am. What I want.

Rob was a guy. A kind of fucked-up, unconventional guy, but a guy all the same.

And what he wanted was Dylan.

With the revelations out of the way, he and Mike talked well into the night. About Rob's gender confusion, at first, a discussion that included several apologies for the way he'd misled and mistreated Mike, and just as many expressions of thanks for how cool Mike was being about all this. After that, they mostly caught up with each other, shot the shit about college, that sort of thing. They ended the night by doing a dungeon run together, and the whole time Mike made fun of Rob for being so rusty with his old character.

"Thanks for being my friend," Rob said when it was time for bed.

"Thanks for being mine. So hey, before you log off, can you tell me your real name?"

No hesitation. "Robert."

"Wow, so Bobby must have been a real stretch, huh? You sure are one creative dude."

"Says the guy who named his elf alt after a character from *Lord of the Rings*."

"I believe you will find that Fëanor, son of Finwë is a character from *The Silmarillion*, my friend. Now go to bed. And go to fucking school tomorrow, you slacker."

Even though they weren't on video chat anymore, Rob saluted him. "Yes, sir! Goodnight, sir!"

"G'night, Rob."

The next morning, Rob tried calling Dylan. Straight to voicemail. Not too encouraging, but there was always school. They couldn't really talk over their issues in class, of course, but maybe they could meet for lunch, or go to that pizza place Dylan liked. Anywhere, it didn't matter. They could go anywhere, just so long as Rob got to give Dylan his answer. Hear Dylan's reply.

But when Rob showed up at the Emily Carr campus at quarter to nine, Dylan wasn't in class. He wasn't there on Wednesday, either. Or the Monday after that.

Finally, on the last day of regular classes before exams, Rob got up the guts to ask Doctor Chastity about Dylan's whereabouts. Had Dylan dropped the course or something?

"Oh," she said, stuffing her overheads and dry erase markers into her satchel. "No, nothing like that. He asked for some time off for a family emergency. He's still going to be at the class's final art show. Speaking of which, I've noticed you've been missing a lot of classes, too, Mister Ng. Are you going to have a piece for the show? Because straight talk, if you don't, you're going to fail my class."

Shit. Shitshitshit.

With everything else going on, Rob had totally forgotten the stupid self-portrait-in-an-unfamiliar-medium project. Oh, sure, Doctor Chastity had mentioned it a couple of times, but Rob had been too busy craning his neck searching for Dylan.

"Oh, yes," he lied, with enthusiasm. "I'm just putting the finishing touches on my . . . piece now. It'll be done on time, promise."

Doctor Chastity nodded like a woman who didn't believe one word she was hearing. "Good boy. I can't imagine what it'd be like to have to take this class twice. But I'll tell you, *teaching* it multiple times? Sucks the big one."

Warning received.

Instead of heading to the bus stop like he usually did, Rob went to the open studio, which on this particular day was full of fellow procrastinators putting last minute touches on their final assignments.

At least everyone else in the room could say they'd *started* their various projects. Rob sure as hell hadn't. He scrounged up a canvas and some acrylic paints. A mirror.

This was his chance, he realized. Dylan would be at the show. This project could serve as Rob's answer. To Dylan's question, but to the whole world, too. His sister, his roommates, his professor, his indifferent classmates. He'd tell them all, and he wouldn't be ashamed, and he wouldn't apologize.

What was it Dylan had said about pop art? *Love it or hate it, you sure as fuck can't ignore it.*

Rob was tired of being ignored, but more than that, he was tired of ignoring *himself.* He'd been stalling, refusing to put a name to who and what he was, refusing to come out to the people he loved, refusing to give Dylan the straight answer he so desperately wanted and needed to move forward.

And the question wasn't just Dylan's, either. It wasn't just Dylan who needed an answer. Rob may not have been smart enough to voice it, but it was his question, too. The question he'd been asking himself, over and over, ever since he'd first donned a woman's sweatshirt and mascara.

Who am I?

What was a self-portrait, if not an answer to that exact question? He looked down into the mirror and saw two faces looking back.

Rob's determined eyes. Bobby's confident smile.

He was going to need another canvas.

CHAPTER 18

Two hours after Rob had sent the text to Bernice, his first to her in weeks, he finally received a reply.

Fine. I'll go. But only b/c it's ur first real show. I'm still mad as hell at you.

Rob picked up his phone, smiling despite himself. He could just picture Bernice nagging at the phone and pacing her bedroom, the whole time trying to defend never speaking to her baby brother again before finally breaking down and texting back.

He hit reply, forcing himself to stop thinking about his sister's dramatics so that he could be appropriately serious with her. *I understand. Hopefully all will be explained at the show.*

See you at 6, she texted back. Could texts be curt? Based on the evidence in front of him, yes, yes they could, because if anyone could manage such a feat, it was Bernice. The girl was so outgoing and open that her emotions just poured off her, kind or cruel, like an overflow. And Rob most definitely deserved the cruel at this point. He only hoped a gesture of openness and honesty on his end at tonight's art show would maybe swing her mood in the other direction.

He'd invited all the guys to the show, as well. Max and Christian, who were still being extra considerate and careful with him after that night at the store, were quick to say yes. Noah agreed on the condition he be allowed to bring his girlfriend—"It'll give me wicked cred with her friends if I take her on an artsy date, c'mon, pleeease!"—and with everyone else going, Austin begrudgingly agreed, as well. The guy never could stand to be the odd man out. Maybe that was something being in team athletics did to you.

No time to think on it, though, because it was already 4:30 and he was supposed to be at the student gallery early to help with setup.

But first, to get dressed. He tore into his shopping bags from the Chinese mall, looking for the pieces for the outfit he'd put together for the gallery show. Grey wool dress pants, ultra skinny in the calves but flared around the thighs in a style reminiscent of riding trousers, which he paired, of course, with black knee-high boots, although these seemed more fit for a ride on a motorcycle than a show horse. The next item out of the bag was a white cotton shirt that cut close to his body and had a high, narrow collar that he buttoned right up to the throat. Finally, a black blazer with a feminine drape of fabric on one half and a neat, more typical menswear cut on the other. Apropos, Rob thought, especially when he pinned a feather brooch to his chest on the masculine side.

The clothes were totally over the top, showier than anything he'd worn as either Rob *or* Bobby, but that was what he wanted. For tonight, for the rest of his life. To not be ignored anymore. To not *hide* anymore. To walk the fine line between two genders, and fuck anybody who didn't like it, or thought they could use it for their own gains.

He'd made another trip to Sephora today as well. This time, though, he'd told the salesgirl he was buying for himself, and she'd helped him choose black eyeliner and a shiny nude lip gloss. Putting it all together—boots and shirt, jacket and makeup and brooch—transformed him. Not into Bobby, not as Rob knew her, but a boy named Bobby, yes, that seemed distinctly possible. He only hoped Dylan would see him, see his self-portrait, and understand.

He wasn't sure what he'd do, otherwise.

Oh, well. Now wasn't the time for doubts and insecurities, it was the time for action.

Who I am. What I want.

Six o'clock. Rob lingered by his portrait(s), trying not to tap his toe impatiently. He was dressed cool now, after all. He needed to act cool, too, or else he wouldn't be able to pull all this off.

None of the people Rob had invited were here yet, and if Dylan was, he hadn't crossed paths with Rob yet. Probably lurking around his own piece. Or maybe he was late. Or maybe he'd copped out sick and was planning on letting his assignment speak for itself.

There was *someone* nearby, though. One of the cardigan crew, a brunette girl with blunt bangs. She was wearing a navy polka-dot dress with a white cardigan and sunshine yellow tights. Mary Janes. Of course.

"Love your piece," she said, gesturing with her wine glass to the two portraits that hung on the white wall just to the left of where Rob was standing. "What is it, commentary on the preference for sons in Chinese culture?"

"Something like that," Rob said, even though it was nothing like that at all.

"Sorry, you know, I don't know your name?" She tilted her head.

"Bobby," he replied. "Bobby Ng. You're Candace, right?"

She flashed him a bright smile. "Yeah! Well, um, nice to meet you, Bobby. Maybe we'll have more classes together?"

"Maybe," Bobby replied, and watched her float away on a tide of twee.

Bernice showed up in her wake, wearing her go-to Little Black Dress and five-inch heels. Just because she was angry at Rob didn't mean she wouldn't take this opportunity to dress to the nines.

When she finally recognized Rob standing there, the annoyed look fell right off her face. "Rob! Wow!" She rushed forward, clasping him by both shoulders, just about to pull him into a hug before she remembered herself. "Still mad at you, but wow. You look . . . cool! I like it." It was then that her pupils flicked just to the left of Bobby's face, making eye contact with the painting over his shoulder. "Oh, is this yours? It's a pretty good likeness. I didn't know you could pai—"

And now she'd seen the second half of the piece.

"Um, Rob, is this supposed to be me?" She blinked rapidly. "Because it kinda looks like you in drag."

Bobby turned to scrutinize the two side-by-side paintings, one of Rob in one of his usual baggy grey henleys, eyes half hidden behind his floppy bangs, and the other of Bobby, looking beautiful and flirtatious with her hair long and her makeup on . . . all while wearing the same grey henley.

"It *is* me in drag," he said, commenting on it as matter-of-factly as if he'd been commenting on a dime-a-dozen watercolor landscape.

"Oh," Bernice said. "Um, please don't get offended, but I feel like you're trying to tell me something with this and . . . are you trying to tell me something, Rob?"

Bobby took her hand and nodded. "I like dressing up as a girl," he said. No point dancing around it, no point mincing words. "I think I'm both, actually. Guy and girl. I'm still figuring it out, myself, but you're my sister and I wanted you to know."

Bernice was quiet for a while after that, but at last she shook her head and clucked her tongue and said, "You always were an odd one," before she pulled him into a tight, unflinching hug.

"I love you," he said into her shoulder, trying hard not to get teary-eyed and ruin his eyeliner. "And I'm sorry."

"You better be fucking sorry," she replied. "I love you, too."

She stuck nearby after their long hug ended, and was at his side when he gave his roommates the same speech, more or less. Christian and Max were predictably cool with it, thanking him for trusting them with this part of himself, Noah was struck dumb with confusion, requiring his girlfriend Jenny to provide the Coles Notes version. Austin wasn't quite so understanding; when Bobby had finished speaking and Noah had finished asking his fifty questions, Austin gave a big, put-upon sigh and cried, "Are you fucking kidding me right now?" to the ceiling, before storming off in a huff.

Noah may have been completely fucking lost on the difference between sex and gender and gender identity and gender presentation, but he had the sense to glare at Austin as he went. "Don't mind him, Rob," he growled, "I'll straighten the fucker out, or else he can find a new place to stay." With that, he stalked off in the direction Austin had gone, leaving Rob standing with his sister, Christian, Max, and Jenny.

"There's something else," Bobby said, and took a deep, fortifying breath. "Christian, I'm ready to talk to you about what happened at the store that night, now."

"Sure," Christian said. "Of course."

"Yeah. Let's hear it," someone else said.

Dylan.

Bobby's gaze was drawn to him, even though he was terrified about what he'd see. He *missed* Dylan, missed his jokes and his body and the way he saw the world, the way he talked about art, and somehow all of that feeling had translated into this insatiable desire to just see his face, and he wouldn't feel so lonely anymore.

Of course, it didn't happen like that at all. Dylan looked much the same as always, but there was a wall between them, Dylan closed to Bobby in a way he'd never been before, not even when they'd first met.

Even so, Bobby looked right at him, expression neutral, forcing himself to push through the hurt he felt at the wary, distant anger he got back in return. "I'd been dressing up as a girl for all my shifts. This customer assaulted me one night." Dylan's eyes widened in horror, but Bobby soldiered on, even though his voice shook. "When he ... g-groped me, he figured out I wasn't, um, what I first appeared, so he blackmailed me. Said he'd tell all you guys about Bobby if I didn't do what he said. That night I called you, Christian, was the night he tried to assault me again. He made me lock the door and go into the peepshow booth where the cameras couldn't see and I think he planned on—" Bobby didn't want to say it. Didn't want to relive it, not even in the most clinical language possible. He was already trembling slightly. "But now I've told you all myself, see, so now he doesn't have anything on me anymore."

"Oh, baby," Dylan said, frowning deeper than Bobby had ever seen him do before. He stepped forward, opening his arms, but not coming close, not without permission. "And then I came in and ragged on you like a total fucking tool. That conversation was the *last* thing you needed right then and I—shit, baby, I'm so sorry. I should have fucking known something was up. You were so shook up and he was so fucking sketchy and creepy and—"

"You had a right to be angry," Bobby said, and walked right into those open arms. Dylan's big strong body sheltered him, absorbing the shockwaves of Bobby's trembling like the rock he was. "I didn't have an answer for you then—I'm not sure if I even have a totally clear answer for you *now*—but I think you do have a right to ask, and at least be kept up to date with where *I'm* at on the whole thing. Especially since I want you to be mine for keeps."

"For keeps," Dylan echoed. "Mine."

"Yeah, like Pogs," Bobby said, and that made Dylan's whole body shake with a slowly building laugh. "Except I won't throw you in the trash a year from now when Tamagotchi comes out."

"Heartening. Thanks." Dylan kissed his forehead, just like that very first time. "So this new getup, this makeup, these portraits. Is this you, then?"

"That's right. Bobby Ng. Flamboyant, femme, part-time girl, but all guy where it counts."

"Good enough for me," Dylan said, and kissed him again for *real*.

"So that's where you've been slinking off to lately," a woman's voice said, and when Dylan pulled away, there was a middle-aged white couple standing there, looking on. "Your . . . boyfriend, Dylan?" the woman asked.

Dylan caught his breath and ran a hand through the hair at the top of his head. "Yeah. Mom, Dad, this is Bobby. He's totally wholesome, other than the cross-dressing." He grinned. "Bobby, this is Sheila, my mom, and Drew, my dad."

Dylan's parents both shook Bobby's hand in turn, and they didn't look the least bit bothered or weirded out, which won them instant points in Bobby's book. Not to mention they'd raised Dylan, which was a win in and of itself.

"I'm Max, and this is Christian," Max introduced, shamelessly butting in. "We're the little guy's roommates."

"And I'm Bernice, *Bobby's* sister," Bernice said, with a smile at Bobby. "But I think I'm going to have these two freshen my drink, now." With one last wink at Bobby, she hooked an arm in one each of Max and Christian's elbows and led them away.

Drew watched them go, then clapped a hand on his son's shoulder. "Now, Dylan, maybe you could show us *your* piece? Since that's why we're here, after all?"

"Have you seen it, Bobby?" Sheila inquired.

"No, ma'am." Bobby didn't miss a beat when she took his elbow. "But I am most certainly looking forward to it. I'm sure it's a showstopper."

"Not compared to yours," Dylan said. "But I like to think I fulfilled the requirements of the assignment. In my own way."

"You're a very dapper young man," Sheila said as they made their way through the tangle of people. "Maybe you could take Dylan shopping?" She nodded toward her son, walking ahead of them with his father, wearing ripped jeans and a red plaid button-down. At least it wasn't flannel.

Rob thought the grunge look was actually pretty sexy, but he knew of at least one thing about Dylan that he'd gladly change. "New shoes. Top of my list."

"Thank God."

There was a buzzing crowd around Dylan's piece, and Dylan had to yell, "Move along, move along, artist coming through!" to get them to make way.

And no wonder there was a crowd. Dylan's piece was huge, five feet high at least, a collage assembled from blown up fragments of old comics, a bright nod to Lichtenstein. The background of the collage was one of those old jingoistic forties covers of a caped superhero battling a massive dictator figure who had two clawed hands wrapped around the globe. But whoever the villain had once been—Hitler or Hirohito—his face was now plastered over with a pastiche of other images, fragmented pieces creating a greater whole: Eskimos and Indians from ice-cream advertisements and sports teams and Wild West strips, parcelled out and reconstituted together in a strange new shape. The resulting figure wasn't so much a menacing one as he was gleefully disjointed, absolutely unapologetic about the fact that he didn't fit together right, that he didn't make a lick of sense.

"What do you think?" Dylan asked, and Bobby was charmed by the note of uncertainty in his usually confident voice.

"I don't get it," Drew said.

"It certainly is . . . well, it draws the eye, doesn't it?" Sheila added.

"Love it or hate it, you sure as fuck can't ignore it," Bobby whispered with a conspiratorial smile, so close to Dylan's ear he could almost kiss the lobe.

Dylan beamed back at him, shaking his head like he couldn't believe this wasn't a dream. "I fucking love you," he replied . . . at full volume.

"I like this androgynous goth look on you," Dylan said, on his knees and opening the many black buttons fastening the fly of Bobby's wool pants. They were back in Bobby's room together, for the first time in what felt like weeks, a little buzzed from the wine and a lot buzzed from the night's revelations. Dylan kissed Bobby's erection through the fabric of his boxer-briefs.

"Thanks," Bobby replied on a moan. "I don't know how long I'll stick with it, though. I'm . . . experimenting."

"Hmm." Dylan used both hands to frame Bobby's dick, stretching the fabric of Bobby's boxers taut so that a clear outline came into view. "Just with clothes?"

"And makeup," Bobby said. "Just a little guyliner, though. Maybe some nail polish. And jewellery."

"What about a piercing?" One of Dylan's hands wandered up Bobby's bared stomach, up under his unbuttoned shirt to tweak his nipple.

"Ah! Nothing permanent. No body alterations."

"No hormones?" Dylan asked, going serious.

Bobby shook his head. "No way. Not for me. I might grow my hair out though." He liked the thought of that, having shoulder-length hair of his own. A more lasting commitment to his feminine side, and no more extensions to worry about clipping in and caring for.

Dylan growled into Bobby's crotch, the combination of sound vibrations and hot breath making Bobby's dick twitch. "More for me to pull."

"Don't even think of it," Bobby warned, but even though they'd gone back to joking, he couldn't help but ask, "So this is okay? Me? Being the way I am?"

"I dunno, am I okay, being the way I am?" Bobby couldn't tell for the life of him whether Dylan was being serious or not.

You're absolutely perfect just the way you are, just so long as you're mine. He stroked Dylan's cheek, cupped his jaw, then gave him a quick little tap on the cheek, just enough to make him jump. "I'm dumping you if you lose any weight. Oh, and also, you could probably stand to learn a little bit of tact."

There was a look of challenge in Dylan's eyes, dark and irreverent and playful, everything Bobby loved about him and more. "Never happening, Puny. I am a man whose mouth cannot be tamed."

"Oh, I think I know a way to tame it." Bobby reached down with both hands and yanked his underwear down, freeing his needy cock and balls. "Open up."

Dylan smiled up at him, eyes twinkling mischievous. "All guy where it counts, indeed," he praised, opened his mouth, and went down.

That night, Bobby did indeed tame Dylan's mouth.

Twice.

CHAPTER 19

Bernice pulled her compact mirror out of her purse, using it to give her makeup a last-minute inspection, then offered it to Bobby so he could do the same. He shook his head at her, gesturing to his room's full-length mirror with a smile.

"So who's this party for, again?" she asked as Bobby turned back to his mirror and rubbed at a smudge in his eyeliner. As he'd expected, Bernice hadn't cared who the party was for or where it was being held or even who was going to be attending, only that it was a party and that she'd be going with her brother.

"Dylan's sister Tina," Bobby replied patiently. "She's retiring."

Bernice whistled. "Retired? How old is this chick, exactly?"

"Um, twenty-six?"

Bernice returned her compact to her purse with a shake of her head. "Retired at twenty-six. Damn, why can't I have her life?"

"I thought you wanted Paris Hilton's life?"

"Yeah, but I think she still works. Well, if you consider being paid to go to parties 'work.'"

"Okay, point, sort of, but still. Tina's, um, not actually *retiring*, per se, she's changing careers." Bobby's own natural tendencies toward privacy and secret-keeping made it tough, but it would be worse to spring it on Bernice at the party. And it wasn't his secret to keep, anyway. It was Tina's life and she'd made a point of being open, just like her brother. "Getting out of porn. It's a whole lifestyle and has its own culture, so leaving is a pretty big deal."

"Oh," Bernice said.

"That's not a problem for you, is it?" Bobby asked carefully, watching her out of the corner of his eye. "Her being in porn?"

"No, oh God no! No no no. You could have told me earlier though, damn. I'd have worn a push-up bra." She squished her breasts together in illustration.

Bobby rolled his eyes. "You look just fine."

"Sure, you say that now, but put me next to a porn star and I'm going to look like the Vancouver chapter leader of the IBTC—you know, the Itty Bitty Titty Committee? You can be the secretary if you want." She gestured to Bobby's chest, where underneath his tight long-sleeved top he was wearing a bra of his own. Another of his experiments.

Having her not only acknowledge it, but accept it, was probably one of the most wonderful feelings Bobby had ever experienced, not that he showed it. "It's a party, not a wet T-shirt contest."

"A party for beautiful people," Bernice said with a pout.

"You *are* beautiful people, Bernie."

She looked to him, eyes soft. "You are too, Bobby."

Despite all of Bobby's attempts to the contrary, a long sappy hug seemed imminent, but then the doorbell rang—or, well, made that sickly *doooo-wong* noise the old thing had a habit of making.

The spell broke. Bernice took one last second to fluff her hair, and then they headed out.

Austin's room was closed up and silent as they passed; the guy hadn't moved out, but he'd definitely been scarce since the night at the gallery, and as much as Bobby told himself Austin's opinion didn't matter, it still hurt. Well, it wasn't like Bobby hadn't done his fair share of hurtful things. Maybe Austin would come around.

When they got down the stairs, Dylan was standing by the open front door, wearing a black button-down shirt, jeans, and—yes!—new shoes.

He waved at them both. "Hey, Puny! Hey, Bernice! Ready to go?"

"Just gotta get my shoes on," Bobby said, and pressed a kiss on Dylan's mouth.

Dylan hummed with pleasure, then pushed Bobby back to arm's length and got a good look at him, brushing some stray hair out of Bobby's eyes. "You look great. You guys are going to love my sister, especially you, Bernice, I think she's a lot like you." Which made perfect sense in Bobby's mind, because if Bernice had ever done porn, she'd probably throw a party when she moved on to other things, as well. Okay, Bernice wouldn't even need that as an excuse to throw a party.

How times had changed. Once upon a time, Bobby would have been terrified at the idea of going to a big party for a woman he didn't know, especially considering the fact that Tina probably had a pretty colorful friend group. But now he was buzzing with excitement. Genuinely looking forward to the evening ahead as he laced his suede ankle boots.

As excited as he was, though, the reality of the evening was ten times better, because waiting for them at the curb was a stretch limo.

"Oh my God!" Bernice shrieked, and immediately put on her red carpet impression as she made her way down the front path—easier said than done when you took into account how badly damaged their yard was.

Bobby looked to Dylan in silent disbelief, and Dylan just shrugged. "She said she wanted a party. Never does anything halfway, Tina. Also, I think she's making up for the fact that she didn't get one at prom."

Free limo ride. Bobby wasn't going to waste time questioning it. He took Dylan's hand and followed Bernice across the yard, then climbed into the car after her.

Inside, the limo was huge and swanky as fuck, with leather seats and a light-up ceiling. Someone pushed a glass of champagne into Bobby's hand before he'd even sat down. Dylan's parents, Sheila and Drew, were sitting across from him, and beside him, the one who'd put the glass in his hand . . . must be Tina. She was a striking woman, tall as her brother and just as round-faced, but with sharper features and glossy black hair that fell to her elbows.

"You must be Bobby," she said as the cab pulled out into the road, and something about the soft, careful way she spoke seemed to resonate in Bobby, like there was a word on the tip of his tongue he couldn't quite remember.

"And you're Tina," Bobby replied with a bob of his head, but there was that feeling again niggling at him, a scratch right in the center of his back. "This is my sister, Bernice. She never passes up a party."

"*Also*," Bernice said, crossing her legs with a dramatic swing, "These two owe me one after they stood me and my girlfriends up at Celebrities last month."

"Dylan stood somebody up? Color me surprised." Tina laughed, then pursed her lips and raised her glass. She conspicuously looked for something to tap it with, but eventually settled on using her acrylic nail. "Anyway, I know you all think I'm the type of person to just rent out a limo for kicks, but I actually have a pre-party announcement to make and I wanted all of you here for it. Well, except for Bernice, of course. No offence. Not that I mind you being here, but I hadn't planned on it."

Bernice smiled. "Don't worry about me."

"Oh, I'm not planning on that, either. Anyway, so I have some big news. Just before I crossed the border, I got a letter from the BC health plan people saying my psych evaluation has been approved. I'm scheduled for my gender affirmation surgery in Montreal next year!"

Before Bobby could even process what she'd said, Dylan whooped and Sheila let out a squeal and enfolded her daughter in her arms.

"That's amazing!" Dylan said. "And the government's going to pay for it?"

"Everything but the airfare and the recovery time in hospital," Tina said with a rapid, ecstatic nod. "And I think I've got enough saved up for that."

"Well, if not, you have a year to save," Sheila said.

"Or your mother and I can just pay the difference," Drew added.

"Dad!" Tina dabbed at the tears in her eyes. "You're the best. The absolute *best*."

Gender affirmation surgery. She's trans. It all clicked, and suddenly absolutely everything made sense. Dylan's sensitivity to Bobby's issues, his knowledge, the way he'd been so tentative to touch Bobby in certain ways. Every single assumption he'd made. He'd watched his sister walk this path, probably from the beginning, and had seen something of the same in Bobby that led him to believe that Bobby would follow her, sooner or later.

He was happy for her. Happy for Dylan, who was incandescently happy for her.

But no, he would never follow her.

Even growing up as Bernice's brother, Bobby had *never* seen a party quite like this. An entire hotel ballroom space rented out for something other than a wedding or a funeral, and not only that, actually stuffed to the gills with people. He'd thought Tina might have colorful friends, but none of his preconceptions could have prepared him for the infectiously happy crowd that Tina surrounded herself with.

Diverse would be an understatement, and Bobby *loved* it. His roommates all (mostly) loved him, and so did his family, but he was still always the odd one out, and that was a feeling that no amount of acceptance and kindness could quite make up for. But not here. Gender here flowed along a mad and amazing spectrum, from drag queens in pink wigs and four-inch platforms to genderqueer people in trim, tailored suits. Tina and Bernice had gotten on just as well as Dylan had predicted, and the pair of them had been absorbed by the motion and the rhythm of the crowd, becoming a part of the wonderful chaos.

For Bobby, it was loud and incredibly overwhelming, but Dylan stayed by his side the entire time, his arm safely tucked around Bobby's waist but never steering him.

"What do you think?" Dylan asked in Bobby's ear after an hour had passed in a bass-thumping multicolored blur.

"Amazing!" Bobby shouted back. "Your sister must be super popular, I've never seen this many people at one party."

"She has a real cult of personality," Dylan agreed with a nod. "Better watch out or your sister will become a worshiper!"

How strange that Dylan and Bobby had both grown up so similarly, in the shadow of a glittering older sibling, but Dylan had turned out so *different*. Bobby might have been bitter about that, once upon a time, bitter that he couldn't have handled his shit better, but now all he felt was happy that he and Dylan understood and complemented one another so well. He couldn't ask for much more than that.

Except for maybe . . .

Bobby stood up on tiptoes, one hand curling over Dylan's shoulder and the other splaying across his broad chest. Dylan, drawn to him, bent down to him almost imperceptibly, but the shift was just enough to put Bobby's mouth at his ear. "It *is* a little loud in here for me," Bobby murmured, and when Dylan looked at him, eyes widening and eyebrows rising, Bobby bit his lip to seal the deal.

"You wanna get out of here?" Dylan replied, and sure it was a total line, but not with Dylan's breathless delivery, like he was genuinely *surprised* that Bobby would be interested in him.

"I may have been hinting at such a thing." Bobby nudged Dylan with his hip.

"You may have? Well, I don't know if 'may have' is quite compelling enough for me to put my neck out there by telling you I have a room upstairs for us."

"You what now?" Bobby gaped, completely dropping the coy act. Wow, he'd been gunning for them to relax their scruples enough for a blowjob in a bathroom stall, but a hotel room?

Dylan laughed, clearly pleased with himself for being able to surprise Bobby. "C'mon." He took Bobby's hand.

They made it as far as the elevator before they were making out, which also just happened to be where Bobby learned that yes, making out with your legs around a man's waist while he pressed you to a wall was hot as hell . . . but not advisable against elevator doors, which, of course, opened without warning behind you and left you both toppling onto the elevator floor.

Bobby also learned that making out on an elevator floor with a bruised ass and head? Still great.

So was stumbling down the hall together still tangled in one another's limbs, bouncing off walls because you were too busy kissing to pay much attention to where you were going.

But none of it was as good as finally falling through that hotel door, into a generic two-bed room that was somehow wonderful just by virtue of being *yours*. Once the door shut behind them, though, Bobby snapped back to his senses and broke off the kiss with a gasp. "Dylan. Dylan. Just let me go into the bathroom and get naked, 'kay?" He squirmed in Dylan's arms, but Dylan wasn't letting go.

"Why not here?" Dylan asked.

Bobby blushed. "Girl underwear. Let me just get rid of it, okay?"

"You don't have to do that." Dylan took Bobby by the shoulders and held him still.

"I do. Look, you've been really cool about all this, but I don't want to . . . make you uncomfortable with this whole bra-and-panties thing. You like men. I want to be a man for you. Just give me a second." Bobby hadn't minded, but vocalizing it aloud made his throat catch painfully.

"You are a man for me, Bobby." Dylan twisted his lips in frustration, like that hadn't come out right. He tried again: "Man *enough* for me. You're a man who likes pretty little bras—don't think I didn't notice—and pretty little panties and eyeliner, and that doesn't make me uncomfortable at all. I love it."

"What? Really?" Oh great, now the tears were starting.

"Really. When I said I wanted a man, I didn't mean you had to get all butch on me, Puny. I just meant I wanted you to know in your heart you *weren't* a woman, and that you had no plans to go the way of my sister. After that, you can be as femme as you like. I'll still want you exactly as you are. Promise."

"I love you," Bobby murmured, smiling and dabbing his eyes. "I love you so, so much." He hiccupped. Laughed a little.

Dylan's smile was fond. Gentle. It amazed Bobby how gentle a rough punk in an ERASE RACISM sweatshirt could be. "I know, Puny. I love you too." He caught Bobby's chin and tilted his face for another kiss, and then the sweetness shifted to something else, something hotter but no less profound. The kiss deepened. Dylan's hands swept down from Bobby's shoulders, down to cup his tits in their little lace bra through his shirt. "And I'm actually getting into the whole girl thing, to be honest. Hell, lately I've been having this fantasy that we go out, but with you in full girl mode, and you're wearing a short little skirt and at the end of the night I hike it up around your hips and pound you from behind like the pretty little slut you are."

"Oh," Bobby breathed.

"Yeah. Oh. So how about you give me a little preview and take off everything *but* whatever little girly bra and panties you've got hiding under there?"

"I could . . ." Bobby stepped back, back again, back until he was far enough away that he hoped Dylan could see all of him. The flush on his cheeks didn't feel burning or shameful anymore, it felt sweet and warm, and Bobby felt sweet and warm too as he undressed, kicking out of his shoes and shimmying out of his skinny jeans, then button by button shedding his shirt. The bra and panties underneath were white cotton and lace, virginal, in complete contrast with the so-called androgynous goth clothes that had hidden both—not to mention with the erection stretching the tiny panties to their limit.

Dylan said nothing. Neither did Bobby. Bobby didn't even move, just stood there posed like a music box doll, waiting to have his key turned.

And then, "Shit." Dylan shook his head and laughed softly. "Here I was expecting something kinky and you go making me look like a dick, because I'll be damned if this isn't kink, it's fucking art. You're beautiful, Bobby."

"Oh my God, stop," Bobby tittered, covering his face with his hands in a move that was absurdly Chichi Yamaguchi-esque. Except that was an act put on for fetishizing men like Adam, and this was pure and good, and God, he was in love with Dylan, and he wasn't going to think about Adam anymore.

They fell onto the bed together. Dylan struggled to get out of his jeans while horizontal; Bobby focused on the buttons of Dylan's shirt, slowly revealing the warm, smooth brown of his skin. When Bobby reached behind his back to undo his own bra, though, Dylan shook his head. "Keep it on? For me?" Bobby nodded and Dylan reached down to sweep Bobby's hair out of his eyes and kiss him again. "The panties gotta go though, sorry."

"I'd be sorry if you wanted me to keep them on." Bobby lifted his hips and Dylan stripped the panties away. Let them fall to the floor.

Dylan kissed the shadow between Bobby's breasts, mouthed the edging of the lace where Bobby's flesh was just barely plumped by the gel inserts.

One of his hands, meanwhile, strayed lower, down to cup and roll Bobby's balls, and then his middle finger slipped back even farther, petting Bobby's taint with firm, maddening strokes.

Bobby arched, but there was nowhere for him to go, not with that big body bearing down on him. Dylan leaned in close, nipping his earlobe, and whispered, "You want me to fuck that tight little pussy of yours?"

The words were a livewire, charging every single inch of Bobby's body. Every nerve. Every capillary. He moaned and bucked, cock glancing against Dylan's thicker one. "Yes, yes," he groaned back, squirming across the mattress delirious with the pleasure of being pinned in place.

"Show me," Dylan said, and the fingers that had been stroking between Bobby's legs were rubbing his lips instead.

Bobby's response was instinctual: he opened up. Opening himself to a man like Dylan, that was what he was *made* for. He sucked those thick fingers into his mouth, sealed his soft lips around them, held Dylan's eyes as he drew them in deep and then let them glide back again, tracing his tongue.

Dylan's voice when he spoke was gravelly, primal. "Making it hard for me not to put my dick in your pretty mouth—" Bobby moaned. *Yes, yes, let me suck you. Let me be pretty for you, let me be yours.* "— but I promised to fill your pussy tonight, and a promise is a promise." He pulled his fingers free of Bobby's lips and squeezed Bobby's breast with his opposite hand and suddenly there were wet fingers between Bobby's legs, skirting back, teasing Bobby's hungry pussy. He threw his legs around Dylan's waist—opening himself, always, always, receiving, he was the receiver—and at last Dylan's fingers sank inside him, stretching painfully, making his claim.

Bobby gave Dylan his pain, gave Dylan the root of his pleasure, gave Dylan *everything*.

And how strange and wonderful was it when Dylan gave back— openly, unflinching—everything of *himself*, too. "Ready for me, my pretty girl?" he asked into Bobby's ear, hand wedging up underneath Bobby's bra to flick his nipple. *Always. Anytime. Forever.*

They separated a moment, and then Dylan was back again, hand slick now, stroking every sensitive inch of Bobby's skin between his legs from his balls right back. This time he spent so long teasing, so long tickling and rubbing, that when at last one finger breached Bobby again, he cried in surprise.

"Doesn't hurt, does it?" Dylan asked, bringing Bobby back to Earth again with the steady frankness of his words.

"You'll have to do better than that," Bobby retorted, and to prove it grabbed Dylan's questing hand and shoved a second finger into his body alongside the first. Dylan grinned at him, pleased by his forwardness, but oh, it wasn't enough, it wasn't nearly enough, not for Bobby. He sucked his two first fingers, tasting of pre-cum—had he been touching himself with them? Dylan, maybe?—and when they were just wet enough, he reached down, forcing them in knuckle-to-knuckle with Dylan's.

Together they had four lubed fingers pressed into Bobby's wet, aching pussy. A stretch just on the edge of too much, and Bobby loved it. Could take it.

And when Bobby was wild with need, he wrapped his legs around Dylan's hips again, pulled him close. And with his still-slick fingers tucked between Dylan's ass cheeks, teasing his hole, Bobby opened up once more, this time to take Dylan's hard, sheathed cock.

Dylan bit Bobby's shoulder and speared him in one smooth stroke, took him and conquered him until Bobby could do nothing but scream into Dylan's chest and scrape his nails down Dylan's back.

They fucked hard. Held nothing back, reserved nothing, kept no secrets.

No secrets. Bobby hadn't imagined such a thing was possible, but there it was, complete honesty between them, and it wasn't frightening or humiliating or weak at all. Vulnerable, yes, but empowering too, and so very, very sweet.

Dylan had taught him that.

Dylan, who was now rearing up above him, breaking the film of sweat that joined their chests, who now looked down on Bobby from above, *watching* him as they fucked. Bobby was sure he was a mess, hair tangled, lip gloss smeared, eyeliner smudged, face a mask of pleasure and pain, but he wasn't ashamed, not in front of Dylan, not anymore.

No apologies. No explanations.

No secrets. No shame.

He was free.

CHAPTER 20

B ut Bobby wasn't free, not quite, not without this one last thread tied up. And so, a week later, he returned to Rear Entrance Video for what may well have been the last time.

And waited.

Two hours later, the bell over the door jingled. Bobby closed his eyes and counted to ten.

Right on time.

"Well, well, well," Adam said as he stepped inside the door, locking the deadbolt with a loud, final click behind him. "Look who it is. Kept my number all this time, did you, baby? I knew you were drooling for the D."

"Your number's in the store system," Bobby snapped.

"But you *are* drooling for the D." Adam flashed a cocky—ugh—grin and flopped an arm onto the counter flirtatiously. Did he seriously think he had the right to *flirt*, after everything he'd done? Of course, he probably just saw it as being persistent, not . . . Bobby gulped. He needed to not go there, not now, not if he wanted to be strong and pull this off. Acknowledging it for what it was still shook him up a lot, threw him back to that terrible moment. Better to not even think about it. "So what happened to that boyfriend of yours? He ditch after he found out you were a ladyboy?"

"Nope," Dylan said, emerging from one of the peepshow booths cracking his knuckles. "He's right here. And he's seriously considering kicking your ass."

"Dylan! We agreed no violence." Christian popped out of the second booth, wearing his sternest teacher face.

Adam spun on his heels, looking around the room like a cornered animal. Which he kind of was. Especially now that Noah, Max, and

Christian's aunt Beverly had also emerged from their hiding places. "What the fuck?" Adam shouted.

"But his face is just so punchable," Max said. "And hey, I can kill two birds with one stone and pretend his face is Austin's for at least a couple hits."

"Max!" Christian protested helplessly.

Auntie Beverly stepped forward, putting back her shoulders. "Boys, Christian is right. No violence." She looked straight at Adam, who still seemed unable to process what, exactly, was happening here. "We just want to talk to you."

"You guys are threatening me. I'm calling the cops. This is fucked."

Beverly shook her head. "I don't think so. You see, I went through the store's security footage the other night, on the days and times Bobby told me to check. I'm sure you thought you were smart, forcing him into the peepshow cubicle, but we still have you on camera grabbing him and harassing him. There's no sound, but your body language is pretty clear. I wonder what the police would think of that?"

Adam turned to Bobby now, but surrounded by his friends, Bobby didn't find Adam's furious expression nearly as threatening as before. "You wouldn't," Adam said.

Bobby didn't flinch, and his voice was soft and calm. "I don't want to." Too much hassle, too much humiliation.

"And I support his choice," Beverly said. "We *all* do, don't we, boys?"

Bobby's friends all nodded their agreement, even if Dylan didn't look particularly happy about it.

Adam was thoroughly confused now. "Well . . . good."

"On one condition," Beverly added, raising a finger. "You leave this store, right now, and you never come back. Not alone, not with your friends, not when Bobby's working, not on his day off. Never. We see you here again, or hear about you causing Bobby trouble at all, anywhere—"

"And we can't be held responsible for what happens to you," Max put in ominously.

Beverly sighed.

Adam was visibly squirming now. "Fine, fine. Can I go, then?"

"Not just yet," Dylan said. "First, you're going to apologize to my boyfriend. Go on."

"Ugh. I'm *sorry*. Now can I go?"

Dylan shook his head and took a step forward, and Bobby couldn't help but feel triumphant at the way Adam visibly flinched. "Try again," Dylan said. "This time like you mean it."

"Yeah, grovel," Noah added gruffly.

"On your knees!" Max let out a mean laugh.

"Ugh, no thanks." Time for Bobby to put this whole farce to bed. He just wanted it over with. Wanted Adam gone forever. "You know what, Adam? I don't even want a shitty apology. Not from you, not if you don't mean it. So just get the fuck out and don't come back. I never want to see you again."

"Oh, I wouldn't worry about that. I'm fucking out of here. Bunch of freaks."

Beverly gave him a cheerful wave. "Don't let the door hit you!"

One last snarl over his shoulder—toothless, it didn't make Bobby feel *anything*, least of all scared—and Adam was gone.

Bobby sighed, breathing all of the tension out of his body. But then, with it went whatever stubbornness was holding him together, because he instantly started to tremble.

Dylan noticed first, and went to him, gathering him tight in his big arms. Bobby breathed in his smell, let Dylan's solidness absorb the tremors like it always did and maybe always would, lips pressed to the top of Bobby's head. "You were amazing," Dylan whispered into his hair. "So brave, my brave—"

"Group hug!" Max shouted, and suddenly Bobby and Dylan were crushed on all sides, arms and chests and defiantly optimistic laughter.

When they at last broke apart, Beverly put up a hand like a school teacher. They all went quiet. "I have something to say. Christian and I have a surprise for you all. Hopefully after you see it, Bobby, you'll feel comfortable staying and working here."

I already am, Bobby thought, but didn't want to interrupt her. *With all of you here, I already am.*

"Christian, would you care to do the honors?" Beverly asked, and Christian grinned ear to ear, going to the filing cabinets where they kept the DVD discs. He opened the empty bottom drawer and pulled out . . . a sign?

CLOSED FOR RENOVATIONS.

"Huh?" Max asked, speaking for all of them.

Beverly looked from face to face. "Well, I've been talking with Christian and Sandra—my partner," she added for Dylan's benefit, "Business and otherwise—and we've decided that there are enough seedy adult video stores on Davie street. We want Rear Entrance Video to be something a little bit more suited to the neighbourhood . . . and safer for our staff. After all, the nature of the store attracts the nature of the customer. The culture of the product sets the tone, and I've come to realize that what we have now isn't what I want for me, my staff, or this community."

She was looking a little teary, dabbing at her shiny eyes with her knuckle, lip wobbling. Christian took over from there. "So we're liquidating about ninety percent of the existing video stock, selling it wholesale to one of the stores down the street, and we've signed on with a queer video and book distributor instead. We'll still be Rear Entrance Video, just . . . new and improved."

"And gay!" Dylan cheered.

"Aw man, so I get to say I work at a queer bookstore, now?" Max pumped his fist. "This is gonna do wonders for my street cred."

Christian nodded proudly. "We're going to sell and rent more by-LGBT-for-LGBT porn like the Mischievous Pictures stuff we already have in stock. And then we're going to add a new section for books and magazines, including erotica and comics. And we're going to start selling some nicer sex toys, too."

"No more corn on the cob vibrators?" Noah asked.

"Oh, we may keep those, they're one of our best sellers." Beverly winked, and suddenly her tears were gone. "So here's to our new future."

"Starting with this." Christian reached behind the filing cabinet and pulled out a sledgehammer. "Bobby, would you like to do the honors?" He held out the sledgehammer at arm's length and nodded meaningfully in the direction of the two peepshow booths.

"With pleasure," Bobby replied, heart bursting with happiness. For him. They were doing this for him. For themselves, too, but for him, because he was a part of them, and they were a part of him. A fucking weird family, but a family nonetheless.

"Damn, let me at it too," Dylan said, clapping Bobby on the shoulder and kissing his temple.

Between the six of them and the sledgehammer, they had both booths reduced to a pile of rubble in minutes.

Later that night, Sandra brought them two huge pizzas and they all sat on the floor together to eat, surrounded by stacks of DVD cases in the process of being reunited with their discs so that they could be boxed up and sold away.

"So will you stay?" Beverly asked Bobby quietly while everyone else was distracted, laughing and shouting at some lewd story Max was telling. Bobby's roommates, coworkers, friends, even his boyfriend, all here for him when it counted, all working together to make him feel comfortable and do some general good in the world. His people. He belonged.

No question about it. "Yeah," Bobby said. "I will. Definitely."

Find more love and laughs at *Rear Entrance Video*:
riptidepublishing.com/titles/universe/rear-entrance-video

Dear Reader,

Thank you for reading Heidi Belleau's *Wallflower*!

We know your time is precious and you have many, many entertainment options, so it means a lot that you've chosen to spend your time reading. We really hope you enjoyed it.

We'd be honored if you'd consider posting a review—good or bad—on sites like **Amazon, Barnes & Noble, Kobo, Goodreads, Twitter, Facebook, Tumblr,** and your blog or website. We'd also be honored if you told your friends and family about this book. Word of mouth is a book's lifeblood!

For more information on upcoming releases, author interviews, blog tours, contests, giveaways, and more, please sign up for our weekly, spam-free newsletter and visit us around the web:

> **Newsletter**: tinyurl.com/RiptideSignup
> **Twitter**: twitter.com/RiptideBooks
> **Facebook**: facebook.com/RiptidePublishing
> **Goodreads**: tinyurl.com/RiptideOnGoodreads
> **Tumblr**: riptidepublishing.tumblr.com

Thank you so much for Reading the Rainbow!

RiptidePublishing.com

also by
heidi belleau

Rear Entrance Video series
Apple Polisher
Straight Shooter

The Professor's Rule series, with Amelia C. Gormley
Giving an Inch
An Inch at a Time
Inch by Inch
Every Inch of the Way
To the Very Last Inch

The Burnt Toast B&B (A *Bluewater Bay* novel), with
Rachel Haimowitz
The Harder They Fall, with Lisa Henry (in the
Rules to Live By anthology)
The Flesh Cartel serial, with Rachel Haimowitz
King of Dublin, with Lisa Henry
First Impressions. Second Chances
Blasphemer, Sinner, Saint, with Sam Schooler (in the *Bump in the
Night* anthology)
Bliss, with Lisa Henry

With Violetta Vane
Mark of the Gladiator
Cruce de Caminos

about the
author

Heidi Belleau was born and raised in small town New Brunswick, Canada. She now lives in the rugged oil-patch frontier of Northern BC with her husband, an Irish ex-pat whose long work hours in the trades leave her plenty of quiet time to write. She has a degree in history from Simon Fraser University with a concentration in British and Irish studies; much of her work centered on popular culture, oral folklore, and sexuality, but she was known to perplex her professors with unironic papers on the historical roots of modern romance novel tropes. (Ask her about Highlanders!) When not writing, you might catch her trying to explain British television to her newborn daughter or standing in line at the local coffee shop, waiting on her caramel macchiato.

You can visit her blog: heidi-below-zero.blogspot.com, find her tweeting as @HeidiBelleau, email her at heidi.below.zero@gmail.com.

Enjoy more stories like *Wallflower* at RiptidePublishing.com!